"What are you saying, Leo?"

"I'm willing to train Jupiter to become a service animal for you. I'm optimistic it can work."

Kit let out a joyful cry. Her hand flew to her mouth to muffle the sounds. "I'm sorry. It's just that this is such incredible news."

Leo smiled. "Never apologize for being joyful."

Kit liked the way Leo Duggan grinned. He had such a tender, comforting vibe about him.

"So, if you're still interested—" he began.

She cut him off. "Of course I am! One hundred percent."

Leo chuckled at her enthusiasm. The little crinkles by his mouth were downright adorable. "Okay, then." He rubbed his hands together. "Why don't we start the day after tomorrow? Bright and early."

She bobbed her head in agreement. "Leo, I can't thank you enough. This is an answer to my prayers."

"I'm happy to help." His expression turned solemn. "I've offered up a lot of prayers that were never answered, so I'm thankful one of yours was."

Belle Calhoune grew up in a small town in Massachusetts. Married to her college sweetheart, she is raising two lovely daughters in Connecticut. A dog lover, she has one mini poodle and a black Lab. Writing for the Love Inspired line is a dream come true. Working at home in her pajamas is one of the best perks of the job. Belle enjoys summers in Cape Cod, traveling and reading.

Books by Belle Calhoune

Love Inspired

Home to Owl Creek

Her Secret Alaskan Family
Alaskan Christmas Redemption
An Alaskan Twin Surprise
Hiding in Alaska
Their Alaskan Past
An Alaskan Christmas Promise

Alaskan Grooms

An Alaskan Wedding
Alaskan Reunion
A Match Made in Alaska
Reunited at Christmas
His Secret Alaskan Heiress
An Alaskan Christmas
Her Alaskan Cowboy

Visit the Author Profile page at LoveInspired.com.

An Alaskan
Christmas Promise

Belle Calhoune

LOVE INSPIRED
INSPIRATIONAL ROMANCE

LOVE INSPIRED®
INSPIRATIONAL ROMANCE

Recycling programs
for this product may
not exist in your area.

ISBN-13: 978-1-335-58538-7

An Alaskan Christmas Promise

Copyright © 2022 by Sandra Calhoune

For questions and comments about the quality of this book, please contact us
at CustomerService@Harlequin.com.

Love Inspired
22 Adelaide St. West, 41st Floor
Toronto, Ontario M5H 4E3, Canada
www.LoveInspired.com

Printed in U.S.A.

Be strong and of a good courage, fear not,
nor be afraid of them: for the Lord thy God,
he it is that doth go with thee;
he will not fail thee, nor forsake thee.
—*Deuteronomy* 31:6

For my daughter Amber.
Thank you for being such a bright light in
my life. Your big heart, sense of humor and ability
to uplift those around you always make you shine.
Love you to the moon and back.

Chapter One

Kit O'Malley gripped the steering wheel tightly as she navigated her tomato-colored truck down the snow-covered Alaskan roads. Last night had brought with it a brief squall, creating a winter wonderland effect in Owl Creek. As the snowy landscape unfolded before her eyes, Kit made sure to soak in all the glorious details. She was determined to imprint the images in her mind while she still could. Sitka trees dusted with white powdery snow. A brown and yellow moose crossing sign. Craggy mountains looming in the distance. She put her foot on the brakes as a family of ginger-colored foxes darted into the road from the edge of the woods. Kit let out a sigh. She lived in one of the most magnificent places in creation. How would she ever get used to living in a world of darkness?

For weeks now she'd been feeling disheartened and uncertain about the future. Not even the holiday season was enough to lift her mood, despite the fact that Christmas was her favorite time of the year. Ever since her daughter had been born, the holiday season was even more special. Her recent medical diagnosis had turned her life upside down so that now all she could think about was losing her eyesight to macular degeneration. Kit didn't believe anything could ever fully prepare a person for such a devastating blow. Since her grandfather had also suffered from the condition, Kit had always worried it might happen to her as well. And now an ophthalmologist had confirmed her worst fears.

She'd confided her diagnosis to her sister, Jules, who'd told her about Leo Duggan's work with service dogs out at the Duggan ranch. Jules had encouraged her to seek out Leo to see if she could adopt one of his canines. Ever since, Kit had been holding on to the idea like a lifeline. Feeling so helpless about her situation was foreign to Kit. She hated the idea of losing her independence along with her sight. *God, I never imagined You would be so cruel. Just as things in my life were coming together I've been dealt this awful blow. Please grant me strength.*

And she hadn't yet summoned the courage to tell her parents. As it was, Rose and Seamus O'Malley were overprotective of their children. This news would crush them and ruin the holiday season for her family. She wasn't about to let that happen. Christmas brought with it a special happiness that hummed in the air around them. For now, she would keep her diagnosis close to the vest. Jules would be her sole confidante until she disclosed the news to everyone else.

Kit blinked away the tears pooling in her eyes. She had never considered herself to be particularly brave, but over the past few weeks she'd been feeling extremely vulnerable and weak. At the moment she needed to focus on the matter at hand—beseeching Leo to consider her request to adopt a service dog. *Please, God. Grant me favor.*

As she approached the Duggan ranch, Kit drove up to a gate emblazoned with a big *D* on it. *The Double D Ranch.* The bronze and green sign hung on a stone pillar, welcoming her into the Duggans' world. A pine wreath adorned with red ribbons served as a festive holiday decoration. Sprigs of mistletoe hung above the gates. It reminded her that Christmas was quickly approaching. A trickle of excitement flowed through her. Given her circumstances, perhaps she should embrace the holidays with gusto and savor every last Christmas tree sighting and holiday gathering. In order to spare her family, she needed to put on a brave face and act jovial. There was no point in ruining the holidays for them. There would be plenty of time to disclose her illness to them before it became evident.

Once she drove past the gates and onto the property, Kit was able to scope out land as far as the eye could see. It was impressive. A huge expanse of acreage stretched out before her. Horses and cows dotted the snowy landscape. She'd only been to the ranch once for a birthday party when she was a child. It has been for her classmate, Florence Duggan, Leo's cousin. Seeing it as an adult gave her a whole new outlook on its grandeur. Kit imagined it would be nice to live out here with all the wide-open spaces and breathtaking views.

She sucked in a fortifying breath. She'd already

begun to notice shifts in her vision. Her ability to see items in her path was worrisome. Nothing was as visually sharp as it once had been. At times like this, her new reality came crashing over her like a rough wave hitting the shore. Soon her eyesight would be even further compromised, and she wouldn't be able to enjoy the Alaskan landscape as she'd always done. Her hands began to tremble at the thought of it. Kit didn't think she was strong enough to endure such a drastic change to her abilities. If only she were braver and bolder like Jules. Her sister had never been afraid a single day in her life.

Dear, Lord. I've been so scared, and I think working with a service dog would make me feel stronger. And not so alone. Please let this work out so that I can feel as if I have a future.

Up ahead on the road, Kit spotted horses standing outside in an enclosure. They were such beautiful animals, she thought, as memories of past riding experiences came to mind. She wasn't certain, but she thought this might be where Leo was working with the service animals. A bright green truck sat outside the structure. Leo's vehicle—a vintage Chevy—was well-known in Owl Creek due to its distinct appearance.

Kit parked her truck outside the stables and stepped down from the vehicle. Her boots made a crunching sound on the mixture of snow and ice underfoot. Several ranch hands were carrying bales of hay toward the barn. She quickly made her way over to one of them.

"I'm looking for Leo Duggan," Kit said. "Is he here?" she asked, hoping her trip to the ranch hadn't been in vain. She'd considered calling, but it wasn't as if she and Leo were friends. Growing up in a small town didn't always mean you were close with all the townsfolk. Although Leo had a solid reputation in Owl Creek, Kit had always perceived him as a bit standoffish. It was a tad ironic since some townsfolk might say the same about her.

The wizened ranch hand jerked his chin in the direction of the stables. "He's in there, Miss, working with his pups."

"Thank you," she murmured, mustering a smile as she headed off to find Leo.

At the mention of the dogs, Kit's heart began to beat a wild rhythm inside her chest. It felt as if pure adrenaline was racing through her veins. What if they were already spoken for? What would she do then? *Be hopeful*, she reminded herself. Kit inhaled a deep breath as she pushed open the doors leading to the stables. Once she stepped inside, the smell of hay and horses rose to her nostrils. An adorable yellow Labrador puppy bounded toward her, enthusiastically wagging its tail as it reached her side.

"Well, hello there," Kit said. She wished she could pet the dog, but she'd once heard that service dogs shouldn't be touched or interacted with. Frankly, she was a bit surprised the pup had run toward her.

"Jupiter, come back here." A deep commanding voice called out to the dog, causing him to run straight back to Leo. With a single hand motion, he had the pup sitting at his feet and gazing up at him with adoration.

Leo Duggan was an attractive man with broad shoulders, sandy-colored hair and hazel eyes. She couldn't be certain, but he appeared to be just shy of six feet tall. He had a rugged build and a dimple in his chin. His eyes had always radiated kindness. *Alaskan eye candy*. That's what her sister, Jules, called him. Kit agreed, although she would never admit it to Jules. Leo was very nice to look at, but she hadn't come to the ranch to admire Leo's good looks or any other man's for that matter. It would only lead to trouble, and she was already up to her neck in problems.

"I'm so sorry if I interrupted your session," Kit apologized. She'd been so eager to find Leo that she hadn't thought twice about bursting into the stables and disrupting him.

"Hey there, Kit," he said, his voice full of surprise. "No worries. I'm not training at the moment."

Her shoulders sagged with relief. She didn't want to annoy Leo before she was able to ask him for a huge life-altering favor.

He knit his brows together. "What brings you out to the ranch? If you're looking for Florence, she's over at the house with the twins." She and Leo's cousin Florence hadn't been close friends since they were teens, which made Kit sad to think about. Dealing with her pregnancy as an unmarried woman had caused Kit to turn inward. Whispers had followed her all over town, and she'd made the decision to keep a low profile until after her baby's birth. As a result, she'd lost a lot of connections in Owl Creek. Opening up a vintage store in town with Jules was slowly turning things around since the townsfolk were flocking to shop at Second Time Around.

She shifted from one foot to the other and jammed her hands into the pockets of her pink winter parka. She didn't need for Leo to see her trembling hands. *Be brave*, she reminded herself.

"I'm not here to see Florence, Leo. It's you that I need to talk to," Kit explained. She held her chin up and met his gaze head-on.

Leo raised an eyebrow. She swallowed past her nervousness. "I heard about the dogs you're training as service animals."

He nodded. "Yes, I'm working with the puppies I adopted from the Owl Creek Dog Rescue. I took in five pups, but they're not all suitable to be in the program."

Kit let out a surprised sound. "Five? You took on five dogs?"

He smiled, causing little crinkles to form around his mouth. "And their mother, Daisy. She makes six." He let out a low chuckle. "Maya and Ace twisted my arm a little bit, but it's turned out to be one of the best decisions I've ever made. They've kept me on my toes. And it's been a worthwhile endeavor."

Maya and Ace Reynolds were one of the sweetest couples in Owl Creek. Maya ran Best Friends Veterinarian Clinic while Ace, a former dog sled racer, now headed the town's dog rescue, a project conceived by his wife.

Leo gestured toward the dogs behind him. "We were just having snack time before I let them loose in their enclosure. They'll run around for a while and tire them-

selves out so I can get some work done around here."
He narrowed his gaze as he looked at her. "So, what
did you want to see me about?"

She began fidgeting with her fingers. "Well, I wanted
to know if I could adopt one of your service dogs." She
blurted the words before she could chicken out. Her
palms were moist, and she felt little droplets of sweat
on her forehead.

Leo cuffed the back of his neck. "I'm sorry, Kit.
The dogs being trained are already matched up with
people who require their services. I conduct the training with the dog and the individual. It's been pretty
eye-opening to see how many townsfolk were open to
the idea. I never imagined so many people needed this
type of assistance."

She was too late! Her heart sank like a stone at the
knowledge that she wouldn't be getting one of Leo's
service dogs. "Oh, no. Is there a way to get on a waiting list?"

"Not really. I only trained four of the dogs and they're
going to live with their new owners soon since they're
close to graduating from the program."

Panic began to settle in. She'd latched on to the idea
of working with a service canine and now it had been
snatched away from her. Kit had done a little research
on the subject, and she knew it was difficult to access
service animals. It might take a long while for her to
submit her medical information and go through the
necessary steps to qualify.

"Why don't you check in with Ace at the dog rescue?" Leo asked. "I know for a fact that they have a bunch of pups there looking for forever homes."

No, that wouldn't work at all, she thought. Kit loved the idea of adopting a rescue dog, but she needed the services of a properly trained animal. And she really didn't have any time to waste. From what she knew about macular degeneration, it could progress rather quickly. As it was, her vision wasn't as sharp as it used to be. She'd taken a pretty rough tumble a few weeks ago that left her with bruises. That was the reason she'd sought out the specialist in the first place. Her sight was gradually going to worsen. Just the thought of it made Kit want to dig in her heels and fight.

She couldn't take no for an answer from Leo. So much hung in the balance. Not just for herself, but for her one-year old daughter, Adaline. She was raising her as a single mother, and due to a horrific bomb blast on the other side of the world, her child would never know her courageous daddy. Kit was now both mother and father. Ada's sole provider.

Giving up wasn't an option.

Leo Duggan didn't have a clue as to why Kit O'Malley had come to the ranch seeking a service dog. As far as he could tell, there wasn't a clear reason as to why she might need one.

But he also knew that appearances could be deceiving. Many disabilities weren't visible to the eye. There was something radiating from her that seemed slightly frantic, as if she might be hanging on by a thread. He hated seeing her in such distress.

Gazing into Kit's wide green eyes served as a reminder of her beauty. With a perfectly round face, high cheekbones and long auburn-colored hair, she was striking. Back in their teen years, he'd nursed a massive crush on her. Leo hadn't ever summoned the courage to flirt with her or ask her out on a date. And he never would. Leo was done with romance. It didn't matter if Kit were stunning or as plain as the side of a barn. He'd been a fool for love once and it had cost him his father's life. Leo wasn't going down that road again. Not even for a woman as special as Kit O'Malley.

"Leo, this is important to me. I'm willing to pay whatever you're asking." The note of pleading in her tone made him feel guilty.

He shook his head. "It's not about money, Kit. This isn't something I'm trying to get rich from. It's what I've been called to do." Leo blew out a deep breath. "I'm so sorry. I wish there were a way to give you one of the pups, but I can't take one from someone else."

A tear slid down her face and she quickly brushed it away. He felt a wild urge to put his arms around her and protect her. But from what? He was still clueless about Kit's situation. Why did she seem so frantic?

"What's this all about, Kit? Why do you need a service dog?" he asked, sensing there were things she wasn't saying. This didn't seem like a random request.

Leo locked gazes with Kit. What he saw lurking in the depths of her eyes startled him. A mixture of anxiety and fear. Her lips trembled. More tears glistened in her eyes.

"I'm losing my sight due to an eye disease called

macular degeneration," she said in a halting tone. "I don't just want one of your service dogs as a pet, Leo. I need one."

A shocked sound slipped past his lips. Leo didn't even try to mask his surprise. Kit's news was startling. And deeply upsetting. "I'm so sorry. I know this must be devastating for you."

Kit ducked her head. "It is. I'm already starting to have changes in my vision, but I want to be prepared for when my eyesight really starts to decline. Getting one of your service animals would be incredible. A lifeline of sorts."

Leo had known Kit his entire life, but lately she'd felt almost like a stranger to him. He couldn't even think of the last time they'd had a conversation or even exchanged pleasantries in passing. It had been a long time since they'd attended each other's birthday parties or sat in the same cafeteria. And now she was sharing personal details with him regarding a serious medical condition. It was a bit unnerving, but his heart went out to her. He couldn't imagine grappling with the news, especially as a new mother.

He wanted to tell Kit that he knew what it felt like to have the bottom fall out of one's world, but he couldn't find the words. It was still so hard to talk about the two tragedies that had befallen his family. The loss of his father and his cousin, Ethan, followed so closely by his relationship with Dahlia blowing up in his face still felt like he'd been kicked multiple times in the stomach. Perhaps it would be insensitive of him to compare his losses to her medical situation. It wasn't his way to share personal details of his life. Instead, he would try to help in any way he could.

"If you'd like, I can give you some resources about acquiring a service dog," Leo said. "It might be a bit of a waiting game, but there are organizations that provide them to you after you've gone through a screening process."

If anyone had told him a year ago that he'd be training a bunch of Labrador retrievers to become working service animals and giving advice about the process of being matched with one, he wouldn't have believed them. So much had changed in the past few years. Working with the pups and connecting them with folks here in town who needed their services was one of the only bright spots in his life. If he could assist Kit, he would feel less guilty about not being able to pair her up with one of his canines.

"I know," she said with a bob of her head. "From what I've read, the screening process is extensive, which is what I was trying to avoid. I'm not trying to cut any corners, but I want to train with a service dog sooner rather than later." She bit her lip before saying, "I won't take up any more of your time. Please don't tell anyone about my situation. I haven't told my parents yet. I really appreciate you hearing me out, Leo."

"Kit. I—" Whatever he'd planned to say died on his lips as Kit cut a fast path out of the stables, quickly disappearing from view.

Leo's shoulders sagged with disappointment. He'd missed an opportunity to lift Kit up and provide her with reassurance about her situation. She'd been so disappointed about his not being able to match her with a dog. He clenched his hands at the memory of the tears rolling down her cheeks. Why hadn't he tried harder to console her? Instead, Kit had left looking dejected and a bit broken. Once again, he felt powerless, which was the worst feeling in the world. For a solid year, he'd been struggling with his self-image. There had to be some way he could help Kit find a service animal for her particular needs.

Maybe then he would stop feeling so useless. Maybe then he would stop wondering why God had taken Ethan and his dad while his own life had been spared.

Kit wiped away tears as she drove back to town. She was overcome with emotion and struggling with a fair amount of anxiety. She had dared to be optimistic despite her dire situation. But those hopes had fizzled out in an instant. Her departure from the stables had been abrupt, but she hadn't wanted Leo to witness her bursting into tears. Despite everything, she still had her pride.

Everything in her path seemed dreary as she navigated her way over snow-covered roads and past some of the most breathtaking views in all of Owl Creek. The vista barely registered as her mind whirled with questions. What was she going to do now? How was she going to move past yet another setback?

"You're going to pick yourself up, dust yourself off and keep moving forward," she said in a bold tone that belied the butterflies flying around in her stomach. She met her own reflection in the rearview mirror. "You have to be strong for Adaline." Her chest tightened at the thought of her one-year-old daughter. Loveable and feisty, Ada was the center of Kit's life. Everything in her world revolved around her child. Kit was the sole parental figure and that knowledge weighed heavily on her. She'd just arrived at a place where everything was beginning to come together with single mother-hood and her new business venture. She'd been hope-ful about the future. Kit had always wanted to own a vintage shop filled with timeless treasures, and through hard work and sacrifice, she'd made it happen.

Then without warning, the doctor's grim diagnosis had sent her reeling. Thankfully, Jules had provided a listening ear and a shoulder to cry on. She was grate-ful that they'd shared confidences ever since they were young girls. Kit couldn't ask for a better sister.

There was one secret that she hadn't disclosed to Jules. Although she'd pleaded with Kit on several occa-sions to tell her the identity of Ada's father, Kit hadn't told a single soul.

How could she explain to anyone that she'd been so irresponsible and reckless with Owl Creek's golden boy, Ethan Duggan? Leo's very own cousin. A man who had never known he had fathered her precious child.

Chapter Two

After Kit left the ranch, Leo did his best to get Kit's situation out of his head. No matter how hard he tried to focus on the many projects he'd committed himself to at the ranch, he couldn't seem to concentrate without Kit's face flashing before his eyes. She'd been so achingly vulnerable. And frightened. It was obvious she was in pain. He wasn't used to seeing Kit without a sweet smile plastered on her lips.

Usually when he was working on the ranch, Leo was in his element. There was something about Alaska and ranching that gave him a feeling of pure contentment deep in his soul. He considered himself the most fortunate of men to spend his days at his family's ranch. Even during the darkest moments of his life, he'd found solace here with all of the wide-open spaces, the breathtaking views, the horses and his five pups and their Mama.

The sound of tires crunching on the snow stole his attention away from Zorro, the stunning new addition to the herd. The black colt with the white imprint on his forehead had so much promise. Leo had been in his own little world thinking about Kit's request and her situation, so much so that the vehicle's arrival snuck up on him.

He waved as his cousin Florence stepped out of her old Range Rover. She reached into her vehicle and plucked her twin boys out of their car seats before depositing them on the ground. The trio headed in his direction with the boisterous toddlers leading the way. Florence was Leo's cousin by marriage. His Uncle Patrick had raised her after he'd married her mother, Renata.

Leo exited the enclosure, making sure to latch the gate behind him. The last thing he needed was for the boys to slip inside and run around with the horses. They were both adventurous with a tendency to engage in mischief. The twins reached his side and launched themselves at his legs with each boy grabbing ahold of one of them.

"Take it easy, boys," Florence said in a chiding tone. "You don't want to break Uncle Leo." Even though he wasn't technically their uncle, Leo was the closest thing Florence had to a sibling. It tickled him to serve as their honorary uncle. He doubted that he would ever have kids of his own. In order to do that, he would have to get close to a woman and Leo had no intentions of doing so.

Florence grinned at him. "Hey, Leo. We came to check on you since you didn't make it up to the house for lunch. Everyone was looking for you." Every day, his family broke bread together over lunch and dinner. Attendance was expected unless one wasn't at the ranch. Leo enjoyed those moments of togetherness. It made him feel not so alone.

His cousin winked at him. "I think the boys also wanted to meet Zorro. Their granddaddy was talking about the new colt something fierce. It piqued their curiosity."

"Is that right?" Leo asked, looking down at Florence's sons. They both nodded. Even though they were identical, Leo knew instantly how to tell them apart. The boys filled a space in his heart he feared would always be empty. After being deceived by his ex-girlfriend, Dahlia, Leo no longer believed in the dream of settling down with a forever love and creating a family with her. His heart wasn't big enough to run the risk of it being crushed again. He'd decided to dedicate himself to the Duggan clan and stuff all his previous hopes into a deep dark hole. That way Leo would never have to nurse a shattered heart again.

"Horsey," Jace said, pointing to the corral.

"Giddyap," Carl said, jumping up and down. Leo let out a laugh along with their mother. At a young age, the twins were proving themselves to be mini Alaskan cowboys.

"I get the hint, guys," Leo said, scooping the twins up into his arms. "Why don't I take you on a short ride with Zorro's mama? You can ride together. Does that sound good?"

The twins let out squeals of excitement as Leo headed toward the round pen where Lady was situated. She was the perfect horse for Jace and Carl to ride due to her calm, unflappable demeanor. As a colt, Zorro was too young and unpredictable. For the next twenty minutes, Leo led the boys around the pen, staying close by the mare to make sure they were safe and sound. Florence looked on, smiling as the boys giggled and waved in her direction. Once they finished, the twins began pleading with Leo to see Daisy and her pups, who were in the barn with one of his ranch hands, Ezekiel. After the boys headed into the barn, Florence focused all her attention on him.

"So, what's going on?" she asked. "You seemed a little bit out of sorts when we arrived."

He knit his brows together and let out a sigh. "I was approached by someone who is in desperate need of a service animal. I really felt for her situation, but all of the pups are spoken for. Turning her down didn't feel good."

She let out a tutting sound. "It's not your fault, Leo. I know you have a tendency to want to ride to the rescue, but sometimes it isn't possible." She quirked her mouth. "In that regard, you remind me a lot of Ethan."

Florence's comment took him by surprise. Other than a superficial resemblance, Leo didn't think he and Ethan were alike at all. Ethan's bravery and service to his country had led to his death in action, while Leo had been safely at the ranch. Leo had always felt overshadowed by his cousin. He knew what it was to love someone yet envy them at the same time.

"All of the pups are almost finished with their training except Jupiter. I purposefully chose not to train him."

Florence frowned. "Why not?"

"His temperament didn't mesh well with the program. I wasn't sure it was a good fit."

Jupiter. He was from the same litter as the other Labrador retriever pups, but so far his personality hadn't been conducive to service dog training. At the time Leo began training the dogs, Jupiter tended not to listen to instructions, which was problematic for a service animal. Leo considered him an outlier.

"So maybe you should try again with Jupiter. Maybe now that the other pups will be going home with their new owners, he can focus on commands. It's worth a shot, isn't it?"

Leo scratched his head. *Could it be that simple? Was Florence right?* It was like his father had always said to him. Sometimes you just needed another perspective to find a solution to a problem. "Florence! You're a genius," he said, reaching out for a quick hug before beating a fast path toward his truck.

"Where are you going?" Florence called out after him.

He turned back toward her, mid-stride. "To give hopeful news to someone who isn't expecting it." Leo jumped up into his truck and revved the engine before roaring off down the road. Pure adrenaline was racing through his veins as he made his way into town. He wasn't sure if his plan would come to fruition, but he was determined to give it his all.

Kit paused to admire the holiday-themed decorations in the window of Second Time Around. Candy canes and festive nutcrackers. A miniature Christmas tree adorned with dazzling silver and gold ornaments. An eye-catching red antique sleigh. Decorating the shop's display window had given her immense pleasure. She was a creative person, so seeing her ideas come to life had been gratifying.

As soon as Kit walked inside, she knew Jules would pepper her with questions about her visit to the Duggan ranch. Her sister would be incredibly disappointed on her behalf. She might even head over to the ranch and plead her case with Leo. The very thought of it made her cringe. Kit didn't want to be an object of pity with Leo or anyone else in town. It seemed impossible, but she would just have to swallow her disappointment and forge ahead. Kit turned the doorknob and crossed the threshold of the store as upbeat Christmas music filled her ears. Jules was with a customer, showing her their new ornaments. She locked gazes with Kit, asking her without words how things had gone at the ranch. Kit made a face and shook her head. Jules's hopeful expression crumpled. Kit looked away and began folding holiday sweaters, determined not to give in to emotion while she was on the clock.

By late afternoon, Kit was a bit tired of putting on a brave face. Although she normally loved working at the shop, today felt like drudgery as she attempted to make small talk with customers.

The jangling of the bell hanging above the door heralded the arrival of a customer. "Welcome to Second Time Around," Kit said in her cheeriest voice without glancing up. Even if she didn't feel upbeat, Kit needed to play the part. Everyone expected it during this time of year. Just because she was down in the dumps, it didn't mean she had to pass it along to the next person.

"Thank you," a deep voice said, causing Kit to look up from rearranging a rack of clothes.

"Leo!" Kit exclaimed as he walked inside. A startled sound slipped past her lips. What was he doing here? She had never seen him in her store before this very moment. The timing was odd since she'd recently left the ranch. "I—I'm surprised to see you here." Leo reached her side within seconds, his stride full of purpose.

He took off his dark cowboy hat and pressed it against his chest. "Sorry to just show up here unannounced, Kit, but I need to talk to you and I wanted to do it in person," Leo explained. His gaze was so intense it made her a bit nervous. What was so urgent that he'd come all the way into town to track her down?

She had no idea what it could be, and it made her a little nervous. Kit prayed it had nothing to do with him feeling sorry for her situation. She'd tried her best to hold her head up high during her visit to the ranch. Leo had always been kind and caring. She had no desire to exploit his sweet nature by asking him to reconsider her request. He'd been straightforward with her during her visit to the ranch, which she respected.

Kit knew her confusion must be evident on her face. "I haven't even had time to consider a plan B if that's what you wanted to discuss."

Leo shifted from one foot to the other. "Well, maybe

you won't have to," he said. "I think there might be a solution to your situation."

A solution? Had she heard him right? Kit swallowed past the sudden hope that rose up inside her. Her emotions were all over the place. *Lord, please let Leo have some good news. I can't bear any more disappointment. If so, I'll just curl up into a little ball and cry my eyes out.*

"Why don't we talk in the back?" Kit suggested. A few customers were already glancing over at them with curiosity radiating from their expressions. The last thing she needed was to have them overhear her conversation with Leo about her need for a service animal. Gossip tended to spread like wildfire in Owl Creek and she couldn't run the risk of her parents finding out about her diagnosis before she could break the news to them herself.

Leo nodded, then followed behind her as she led them toward the office she and Jules shared. Kit's nervousness was slightly lessened by the stupefied expression on her sister's face as they walked past her. Jules's mouth was practically hanging open and her green eyes were as wide as saucers. Kit found it comical even though her hands were trembling with nerves.

Once they were both inside the private room, Kit turned to face Leo. His height and broad shoulders seemed to dominate the small space. He towered over her petite frame, but his presence was reassuring not overpowering. Kit was holding her breath, waiting for him to speak. It was so hard to believe that something good might be looming on the horizon. *Have faith*, she reminded herself. *Now faith is the substance of things hoped for, the evidence of things not seen.* Her favorite passage from Hebrews ran through her mind, centering her in this uncertain moment.

"I think I've found a way to get you paired up with a service dog," Leo said, running his fingers along the brim of his black Stetson. A look of satisfaction was etched on his handsome face. As far as she was concerned, his words were a promise.

All the air left her lungs in a single moment as a result of Leo's pronouncement. "Y-you did what?" she asked. Her voice sounded raspy, no doubt from shock. Kit sat down on the edge of the desk for support. Her legs were shaking with anxiety. It seemed as if it were too much to hope for that Leo would have found a way to solve her problem. But then again, if anyone could make something wonderful happen, it was Leo.

"Do you remember the pup who greeted you at the ranch this morning?" Leo asked, unable to contain his excitement.

"Jupiter? Right?" Kit asked, a grin tugging at her lips at the memory of the exuberant pup. As far as she was concerned, Jupiter was the best type of dog— friendly, loveable and easy on the eyes.

He gifted her with a sweet smile. "Yes, that's him. Jupiter was the only pup from Daisy's litter that I didn't train as a service animal." He quirked his mouth. "Because of his exuberant nature, I didn't view the dog as a suitable candidate for the program. Now I'm reconsidering my decision. I didn't give Jupiter a fair shot." Leo let out a regretful sound. "I made the decision based on his temperament, but that wasn't right considering how young he was at the time. Since then I've seen that Jupiter has gotten better at listening to commands. And he's loyal to a fault. That will come in handy."

Kit wanted to ask Leo to talk faster, but she didn't want to be rude. The suspense was killing her! "W-what are you saying, Leo?" She couldn't help but blurt out the question.

Leo inhaled a deep breath. "I'm willing to train Jupiter to become a service animal for you. I'm optimistic it can work."

She let out a joyful cry. Kit's hand flew to her mouth to muffle the sounds. "I'm sorry. It's just that I've been forcing myself to accept what you told me earlier. This is such incredible news."

Leo smiled. "Never apologize for being joyful."

Kit liked the way Leo Duggan grinned. He had such a tender, comforting vibe about him. It made her feel reassured, even though her current situation was still nerve-racking. With his brainstorming, Leo had made her future seem much less frightening. He'd found a way to assist her even though things had appeared bleak.

"On average, it takes a year to fully train a service dog, but he'll come to live with you well before then. It's going to entail a lot of work since he'll be a guide dog. You'll need to be at the sessions several times a week." He seemed to be gauging her wherewithal. "Is that going to conflict with your hours at the shop?" Leo asked.

"Between Jules and I, we'll figure out my schedule."

Her sister would do anything humanly possible to make a path for Kit to work with Jupiter. "It won't be a problem."

"So, if you're still interested—" he began.

Kit cut him off. "Of course I am! One hundred percent." Nothing and no one could stop her from taking advantage of this opportunity.

Leo chuckled at her enthusiasm. The little crinkles by his mouth were downright adorable. "Okay then." He rubbed his hands together. "Why don't we start the day after tomorrow? Bright and early. Then you'll be free to be here at the shop by noon."

She bobbed her head in agreement. "Leo, I can't thank you enough. This is an answer to my prayers."

"I'm happy to help." His expression turned solemn. "I've offered up a lot of prayers that were never answered, so I'm thankful one of yours was."

The way Leo spoke hinted at a secret sorrow. It made her wonder if he was referencing his father's death or Ethan's? Perhaps both. He had endured unimaginable losses in a short period of time. It made it all the more heartwarming that he was bending over backward to try to help her find a service dog. Ever since she'd known him, Leo Duggan had been the type of person who went out of his way to help others. No wonder everyone in Owl Creek adored him. He was such a good guy that it made Kit feel guilty about keeping Ada a secret from his family.

"Well, I should get going," Leo said. "I just wanted to let you know the good news as soon as possible."

"You have no idea what this means to me. I might

actually be able to sleep tonight instead of tossing and turning." Although a service dog wouldn't solve all her problems, it was reassuring to know Jupiter would be trained to help her navigate obstacles and any potentially dangerous situations. He would also be a constant companion for her.

When Leo twisted the door open, Kit heard a familiar voice accompanied by the pitter-patter of little feet coming down the hall. Within seconds, Ada was standing at the threshold, gaping up at Leo with a mixture of apprehension and interest. Kit knew she was biased, but with her light brown curls and blue eyes, Ada was a lovely child.

On many occasions, Kit couldn't help but notice her resemblance to Ethan, all the way down to the dimple in her chin and their shared eye color. It worried her that someone might see the similarities and figure out the truth. That's what happened when a person kept secrets, she realized. Fear hung over you like a dark cloud.

"Well, who do we have here?" Leo asked, getting down on his haunches so that he was on Ada's level. Kit felt as if she couldn't breathe properly as she watched Leo interacting with his little cousin.

Adaline looked at him warily, then took two steps backward. Her child didn't have many people in her life and she seemed to innately distance herself from strangers. She hoped Leo wasn't taking it personally.

"This is my daughter, Adaline," Kit said, leaning down and scooping the toddler up into her arms. Ada placed her chubby hands on either side of Kit's face and kissed her on the lips. Leo appeared to take Adaline's reticence in stride.

"Hi, Mama," Adaline said in a chirpy little voice.

"Hello, sweet pea," Kit said, running her hand over Ada's curls. Her little girl was growing by leaps and bounds every day.

Kit's heart swelled. Although being a single mother was tough, she could never regret this precious life she'd brought into the world. On the rainiest of days, Adaline brought sunshine to her world. She'd taught Kit the most valuable lessons about love and faith.

Her mother watched Ada during the daytime when Kit was at work. But every afternoon she brought Ada to the store so she could spend some time with Kit before they met up for dinner at home.

"She's a cutie," Leo said, holding out his hand so Adaline could make contact. With trepidation, Ada stuck out her hand and brushed it against Leo's. She let out a giggle, then hid her face in Kit's shoulder.

Kit began to pat her daughter on the back in a soothing manner. "She can be a bit bashful at times, but she's a sweetheart."

"Florence lives out at the ranch with her boys, so I spend a lot of time with little ones," he said. Something flickered in the depths of his eyes that caused Kit to wonder if he was yearning for a few kids of his own. She couldn't quite put her finger on it, but within seconds it was gone, replaced by a shuttered expression.

"I really should get going, Kit. I'm happy that I could help you out." A nice and easy grin spread across his face.

Kit shifted Adaline so she was now resting against her hip. "I appreciate you coming into town to tell me the good news." Just knowing she would have this resource made her feel hopeful.

As she stood on the shop's doorstep with Ada waving goodbye to Leo, thoughts of her daughter's father ran through her mind. Leo's cousin had been a great man. Military hero. Owl Creek's pride and joy. Beloved by all. Kit let out a ragged sigh. Although her child was a blessing, the circumstances of her birth were complicated.

She and Ethan had turned to each other for comfort during one of his brief visits stateside. They hadn't been in a relationship. It had been a fleeting encounter. Kit hadn't harbored any romantic feelings for Ethan, and she sensed he'd held no special feelings for her. They'd agreed to stay friends and forget all about their error in judgment. Months after their brief interlude, Ethan had gotten engaged. According to the townsfolk, he'd been blissfully happy and looking forward to the future with a woman named Rebecca. It had been one of the reasons why Kit hadn't told Ethan she was carrying his child. She hadn't wanted to complicate his life or become an object of scorn in her hometown. And then he'd been killed on active duty. Ethan had never known about precious Adaline. She'd waited too late to tell him.

Every time she thought about it, Kit felt a squeezing sensation in her chest. At moments like this, the guilt was almost too much to bear. What would she tell Ada when she was older?

How could she explain all the factors involved in her decision to stay quiet? Kit's stomach twisted just thinking about it. She wasn't sure she could ever forgive herself for robbing Ethan of the knowledge that he was Adaline's father.

Chapter Three

In preparation for his first training session with Kit and Jupiter, Leo woke up at the crack of dawn and fixed himself a bowl of grits with blueberries and brown sugar. After cooking scrambled eggs and a biscuit to go with it, Leo quickly devoured the meal. He considered it a breakfast of champions—hearty and satisfying. It had always been his father's go-to meal before heading out to work the ranch. Leo knew it was one of the numerous ways he was attempting to keep his memory alive. Not that he was good enough to walk in his dad's shoes, but if he could become half the man Wesley Duggan had been, Leo would be content with his life.

He'd been thinking a lot about Kit ever since the morning she'd visited the ranch and requested to work with one of his pups. There was something about her that had always attracted him to her. He'd never had the courage to pursue her, and now, it was out of the question for several reasons. First and foremost, he couldn't bring himself to put his heart on the line again after his humiliating experience with Dahlia.

Perhaps on some level he related to Kit's devastation. He'd endured back-to-back family tragedies and then a romantic heartbreak. Leo still struggled to understand why God allowed bad things to happen to good people. He imagined Kit was racking her brain, trying to figure out why she was going through such a tribulation. In his experience, there wasn't any real answer to the question. But it still didn't stop him from wondering. And asking God for answers.

Please don't tell anyone about my situation. Kit's plea had sounded frantic. It wasn't Leo's place to discuss Kit's diagnosis with anyone, nor was it his habit to gossip. He did wonder why she hadn't told her family about her diagnosis though. From what he'd observed, the O'Malleys were a tight-knit crew who appeared to be loving and supportive of one another. Kit and her siblings had always been well-liked in town. When Kit gave birth to Adaline, Leo had heard whispers about the identity of the baby's father. Although he stayed away from town gossips, Leo couldn't escape the chatter. It made him so angry that people could be so cruel with their thoughtless comments. From what he'd seen with his own eyes, Kit was a wonderful mother. At the end of the day, nothing else mattered. Adaline was a child of God. Precious in His sight.

The loud creak of the barn door alerted him to Kit's arrival. It was just him and Jupiter in the barn, waiting for her to show up. Jupiter ran over to the door without heeding Leo's command to stay put. He let out a sigh.

This might just be the most challenging dog he'd ever trained. Not that he'd trained that many, but Jupiter was different from the rest. He just had to remind himself that with faith anything was possible.

As soon as she stepped inside the barn, Leo had to force himself not to stare. Her baby blue winter parka and matching wool knit cap suited her perfectly. She had a naturally rosy complexion, accentuated by her dark hair and sparkling green eyes. She was lovely.

"Hi, Leo," Kit said, greeting him with a warm smile before turning her attention toward Jupiter. She leaned over and patted him on the head, praising him as she said, "We're going to be great friends, Jupiter. Just you wait and see."

Leo marveled at how upbeat she sounded. It was a huge departure from the other day. He suspected she would have ups and downs on her journey. And he wasn't certain she realized how challenging it would be to train Jupiter. Relying on the dog might just reinforce the realities of her situation. It was always a complex process when a person had to face down their vulnerabilities. He prayed Kit would rise to the challenge.

"A lot of this is going to be about positive reinforcement. Most dogs want to be rewarded for listening and obeying commands. So we're going to work with clicker training, using some of his favorite sweet potato–flavored snacks and a few toys," Leo said.

"Makes sense," Kit said with a nod. "Who doesn't like a pat on the back when we achieve something great? I love getting kudos," she said with a laugh.

The sound of her tinkling laughter brought him

all the way back to childhood and how he'd loved the sound of her merriment. Whether in the playground or in choir practice, Kit had always been so joyful. Leo prayed her medical diagnosis wouldn't dim her light. Life had a way of changing people, especially when they endured hardships. He'd seen it in his own family after Ethan's death. Aunt Ivy and Uncle Jamie still hadn't found their way out of the darkness of grief. Although they were all grieving, Ethan's parents were taking the loss of their son particularly hard. He knew it was tied up in the idea that a parent never expected to outlive their child.

"I'll make sure to give Jupiter plenty of praise," Kit said as she continued to lovingly pat the dog. Jupiter licked her hand in return. It was a good sign that they were getting along so well. Jupiter was a loveable dog, and Leo had a hunch that Jupiter and Kit would make a great team.

Leo nodded. It was nice to see Kit had such a positive attitude. He had worked with plenty of folks in the ranching world who didn't possess the best outlooks. It always made things more difficult in the long run.

"If Jupiter is going to be successful as a service dog, he has to focus on his surroundings, be disciplined, not get distracted and follow commands." Leo knew it might be a lot for Kit to take in all at once, but it was his job to explain things in excruciating detail. This would serve Kit well when she and Jupiter were interacting on their own.

"Sounds like a tall order," Kit said, raising her eyebrows.

Leo chuckled at the expression on Kit's face. "Yes, the standards are high, but he'll be fine," he said. "We're not looking for perfection in the beginning. Just progress." Leo wanted to reassure her while being open and honest at the same time. Training a service dog was work, plain and simple. It wasn't as if you blinked your eyes and ended up with a fully trained animal. Unrealistic expectations could put a wrench in the best training sessions. "Jupiter is a good age to be trained. His siblings were a few months younger when they started. He's got a little maturity on his side, so let's hope that works for your benefit.

"Dogs are really intelligent and Jupiter has shown signs of being willing to learn. He also has a good memory because he always recalls where I hide the snacks." He chuckled at the memory of Jupiter sniffing out his stash spot for treats. This pup had plenty of personality and spunk.

She laughed along with him. "He sounds like a keeper," Kit said. "I'm happy you decided to give him another shot at being a service dog."

"Me too. As a man of faith, it's important for me to believe in things I can't always see," he said with a nod. Sadly, his ability to do so had been seriously affected by being dumped by a woman he'd had deep feelings for. He'd stepped out on a limb of faith and fallen for someone who hadn't returned his feelings. Believing in Jupiter's potential was a whole lot easier than trusting in love. *Never again*, he vowed.

For a few moments, they settled into the silence without speaking. He was standing so close to Kit he could see the little freckles scattered across her cheeks and the tiny scar on her chin. He took a step away from her, knowing he was on shaky ground being in such close proximity to her. Of all the people in Owl Creek that could have sought out his services, why had it been the one woman he'd once had a crush on?

Get your mind out of the past! he warned himself. *Focus on the here and now.*

Leo clapped his hands together. "Why don't we get started? It gets a bit chilly in here so you should keep on your jacket and hat. Gloves would be great too."

Kit fished around in her pockets and pulled out a pair of white mittens. She held them up triumphantly and beamed at him. Being on the receiving end of her spectacular smile caused his stomach to do belly flops. *Easy there*, he reminded himself. This was strictly professional. And even if it weren't, there wasn't any room in his life for romance. He could still feel the hot sting of shame and embarrassment from when he'd come to the realization that he'd been made a fool of by Dahlia. She'd known that he'd fallen in love with her and had worked that knowledge to her advantage to use him as an ATM machine. To this day, the only person he'd confided in about the devastating situation was his best friend, Ace. Telling his family would have been humiliating. He'd been played for a sucker. His pride had prevented him from disclosing the messy details to them, which had only caused the pain and embarrassment to fester on the inside.

He shook off the negative thoughts and willed himself not to go back down that road. Every day he prayed for those memories to fade away into nothingness. So far, God wasn't listening to his pleas. Leo continued to struggle with feelings of humiliation.

From what Leo was able to observe during the session, Kit was a hard worker. Jupiter was a newbie so he'd focused on basic commands. Sit. Stay. Heel. Jupiter had earned treats by completing tasks. A few times, he'd picked up on Kit's frustration and he sensed it had nothing to do with Jupiter. He knew that her situation could lead to depression and a sense of isolation. Bonding with Jupiter would be crucial to establishing a long-term successful relationship between the pair. Leo could still see traces of inconsistency in Jupiter, but the Labrador retriever was a lot more focused than he'd been a few months ago. That was a good sign.

After an hour and a half, Leo detected some fatigue in both Kit and Jupiter. There was no point in pushing either of them too hard on their first day. It would backfire on all of them.

"Why don't we head outside and take a break?" Leo suggested. "It will be good for all of us."

Kit nodded and exhaled a ragged breath. Suddenly, she looked as if she were carrying the weight of the world on her slight shoulders. Worry lines marred her forehead. He could tell something was bothering her, but since they were just getting reacquainted with one another, Leo knew he should tread lightly. Growing up with his younger sister, Tiff, and Florence, had taught him about respecting boundaries with the opposite sex. He needed to be sensitive, considering all she was going through.

Before leaving the barn, Leo reached for his thermos full of hot chocolate and a mug. A warm jolt of sugar and chocolate would reinvigorate both of them. Service dogs learned best with consistency and repetition. Before Kit knew it, Jupiter would be making great strides.

Once they stepped outside, Leo twisted the top off his silver thermos and held it up in Kit's direction. "Hot chocolate?" he asked her.

"Yes, please," she said, waiting as he poured cocoa into the top lid that served as a cup. She eagerly reached for the cocoa, then blew on it before gingerly taking a sip. "This is good," she said. "It's perfect for this weather."

They settled into a companionable silence as they drank the hot chocolate and watched the horses in the enclosure. In a million years, Leo could never get sick of this view—nothing but horses and sky. Jupiter sat at his feet, panting as if he'd run the Iditarod. The dog seemed to be happy.

"I don't mean to pry, but is everything all right? I know we haven't seen each other much since we were teenagers, but I get the feeling you're in your head about something."

She shrugged, then looked away. "I'm grateful that you made it possible for me to work with Jupiter, but—" Kit bit her lip and stopped talking.

"But what?" he asked, sensing she had much more to say.

She stared off into the distance, focusing on the majestic mountain range that dominated the landscape.

"I suppose it's just hitting me that I still have a host of problems to work through. I was so focused on the service dog aspect. Doing so allowed me not to think about the fact that I'm still going to be visually impaired while raising a child and operating a business." She shivered and wrapped her arms around her waist. "I feel like I'm on this little island all by myself, fighting against a tsunami coming straight toward me."

He waited a few moments and let her words sink in. Leo couldn't imagine how overwhelmed she must be. There had been countless times in the last year he'd felt the same way. Sometimes it seemed as if life was so unfair and cruel. "You're not alone, Kit. You have your family, as well as many other people who'll be in your corner. And me. I have your back for what it's worth. I'm going to make sure that Jupiter serves all of your needs. I promise." Just speaking the words caused a tightening sensation in his chest. There was something about Kit that made him feel protective toward her. She was trying so hard to be strong and courageous. He could see how badly she wanted this to work out. How desperately she needed something to ground her in this new reality.

"That means a lot to me," Kit said in a soft voice. "More than you'll ever know. At the moment I'm just feeling pretty helpless." She raised her shoulders in a shrug. "I'm really grateful for the opportunity to work with Jupiter."

"Trust me, it's my pleasure. Matching people up with my pups and seeing them impact lives as service pets is rewarding."

He felt the intensity of Kit's gaze before he turned to look at her.

"I hope I'm not prying," she said, "but this seems personal for you. You said the other day it was a calling. What did you mean by that?"

He ran a hand over his jaw. His throat tightened. It still wasn't easy to talk about losing his dad. "My dad passed away not too long after we lost Ethan. I wasn't ready to say goodbye, but I suppose we never are. I was inspired to start this program as a way to work through my dad's death and to help people with medical issues stay safe. His death isn't something I'll ever get over, but working with the dogs has provided a measure of healing and hope."

She let out a tutting sound. "I'm so sorry for your loss. He was such a sweet man. I remember how he used to pass out sweets in town after Christmas church service. Candy canes and chocolate kisses."

An image of Wesley Duggan's kindly face flashed before his eyes.

Leo tried to smile, but his heart wasn't in it. The ache was still there, resting against his heart. "He always thought of others." He jerked his chin in the direction of the pasture. "He died right over there, working with his beloved horses. He suffered an epileptic seizure and a stroke. I should have been here by his side, but I wasn't. I'll always regret that." He bit down on the inside of his jaw. Even now, he struggled to stop being angry at himself. Leo would give anything to relive that one day.

"You can't blame yourself." Kit spoke in a soft comforting voice. Leo wanted so badly to believe what she was telling him, but he knew it wasn't true.

"Can't I?" he asked in a sharp tone. "I knew he was a bit off that day, but I didn't press it with him when he said that he was fine. So instead, I left the ranch to chase a ridiculous pipe dream. I wasn't here when he needed me."

As soon as the words flew out of his mouth, Leo knew he'd said too much. Kit was now staring at him with wide eyes. Although she was probably wondering what on earth he was talking about, Leo wasn't about to confess that he'd been a colossal fool. All in the name of love.

"I think it's time we headed back inside," he said curtly before turning quickly and heading back into the barn with Jupiter at his heels.

At this point, he would rather have Kit think he was a rude jerk instead of her viewing him as a pitiful excuse for a man.

Kit hadn't expected that training Jupiter to be her service dog would be a cakewalk, but it was proving to be more challenging than she'd anticipated. Jupiter had so much energy, and the training was full of repetition. She would be exhausted by the time she finished her shift at Second Time Around and went home to feed Adaline and give her a bath before bedtime. Spending precious moments with Adaline was the highlight of her day, and it made her feel grumpy that she might be too fatigued to fully engage with her.

Stop whining! she told herself. Working with Jupiter had been an answer to her prayers. At the end of the day, she'd be a fool to block her blessings by complaining. Being here at the ranch was a godsend. If she was just patient and held on to hope, everything would come together in the end. And maybe, just maybe, she wouldn't continue to feel as if she were falling apart.

Leo had snapped at her during their break, which surprised her. He'd always been even tempered, but she'd just seen a side of him that reminded her that still waters ran deep. Clearly, he was carrying around a lot of guilt and anger regarding his father's death. Although she considered it odd to hear him blaming himself for a medical situation, his angst had been palpable. She wasn't going to judge Leo after all he'd been through. The loss of Ethan and Leo's father must've been horrific. Kit knew firsthand about blaming oneself. Not a day went by when she didn't feel ashamed of her choice to keep Ada from Ethan's family.

By the time they'd concluded the session, Leo appeared to be back to his normal self, although a slight tension still hung in the air between them.

Leo got down on his haunches and lavished praise on Jupiter. "Good boy. That was a really solid first session."

Kit held out a salmon-flavored dog snack to Jupiter. Leo had told her to hold on to it until the end of the training to reward the pup. "Sit," Kit instructed, handing over the treat as soon as Jupiter complied. "Well, I'm going to head out. Thanks for the lesson."

"You're very welcome." He shoved his hands in his front pocket. "I'm sorry about being gruff earlier. With

Christmas coming, I've been thinking a lot about my family's losses. That's no excuse for barking at you, but it's the truth nonetheless."

She waved a hand at him. "We all have those moments," Kit said. "I get snappy myself when I'm hungry or thirsty, so thanks for the hot cocoa. You kept me on an even keel."

"It was my pleasure. Are you headed into town?" he asked.

"Yes. I'm doing a shift at the shop, then heading home to Adaline," Kit answered. At moments like this, she yearned to see her little girl. It was hard being separated from her for so many hours. "I'm really fortunate to have my mom look after her so I can work."

"I can tell by the look on your face that it isn't easy to be apart from her," Leo said. His voice was laced with compassion.

Kit nodded. A huge lump was sitting in her throat. "It isn't easy being a single mother. Motherhood is the best journey I've ever been on, but it isn't for the faint of heart. I never imagined I would be raising a child by myself. That's not exactly something little girls dream about." She wrinkled her nose. "I'll never regret having her, but parenthood should be a partnership."

Leo frowned at her. "Is Ada's dad in the picture at all?"

"No," she answered in a trembling voice. "He's not in her life, and he never will be." The question hit her squarely in the chest. Was Leo probing for a reason? Did he suspect that Ethan had fathered her child? Her heart began to pound like a drumbeat in her chest. A part of her wanted to blurt out the truth while the rational portion of her brain reminded her what a bad idea that would be. If she'd wanted to do the honorable thing, Kit would have confessed all after Adaline came into the world. No, she corrected herself. She could have reached out to Ethan while he was alive. But she hadn't. And now his cousin, who shared similar features to Ethan, was causing her to feel unnerved by his steely gaze.

"I really need to get to work," she said, glancing at her watch. It seemed as if she had to bring it closer to her eyes with every passing day so she could make out the numbers. A feeling of panic settled over her. She fought against the sensation of the walls closing in on her. "Bye, Leo. See you next time."

"Bye, Kit. Drive safely," Leo said. "You did good work today. That's something to feel proud about."

Leo's words trailed after her as she quickly made her way out of the barn. His encouragement lifted her up. She hadn't known how much she needed an attagirl until Leo uttered the compliment. It was such a wonderful way to end the first session. Kit needed the validation. She was trying to stay positive when all she really wanted to do was curl up in a little ball and cry her eyes out. Every day it was beginning to sink in more and more that she would soon be visually impaired. How did one begin to accept such a rough diagnosis? How could she deal with losing the freedom to wander all over Owl Creek in her beloved truck? She was beginning to notice even more deficits in her vision. She'd had several falls lately due to her not being able to spot objects in her path. It terrified her to think she might stumble with Ada in her arms. Every day seemed to present more challenges.

Thankfully, she didn't think Leo knew anything about her and Ethan. Surely if he suspected his cousin was Ada's father, he wouldn't be exchanging pleasantries with her. Kit would have seen it written all over his face—the disbelief and anger. Instead, all she'd felt was encouragement and support.

Once she got in her truck, Kit let out a huge sigh of relief. Even though she liked to tell herself she was ready to tell the Duggans the truth about Adaline being a part of their family, at moments like this, Kit knew it was the furthest thing from the truth. She wasn't prepared for a firestorm to surround her precious girl. Although the Duggans were a nice family, it was possible they could try to obtain partial custody of Ada. The very thought of them doing so caused her entire body to quake with fear. Could she run that risk?

It was beginning to sink in that the time might never be right to tell Ethan's family. Maybe it was a secret Kit would have to take to her grave.

Chapter Four

Leo looked out the barn window as Kit roared off down the snow-covered road. So far, her attitude had been amazing, even when he'd been curt with her. More and more, Leo's admiration of Kit was growing. She was exhibiting such grace in raising Adaline by herself. Kit hadn't hesitated to answer his question about Adaline's father, even though it was a bit nosy on his part. Her answer had surprised him. What kind of man turned his back on a child he'd helped to create? It wasn't honorable behavior.

Was he jumping to conclusions? He didn't like to judge anyone. It was possible that it was Kit herself who'd made the decision to cut Adaline's father out of her baby's life. He had to admit he was curious, not in a gossipy manner, but as an old friend who cared about Kit.

It had been a long time since a woman had given him flutters. Butterflies swirled around in his stomach, making him question his sanity. Of all the women for him to feel an attraction toward, why did it have to be Kit? He bit down on the inside of his cheek in an attempt to rein himself in. He had a job to do—to help train Jupiter as a service animal and to empower Kit as her disease progressed. He didn't need the situation to be complicated by his attraction to her. With his dismal track record in the romance department, it would be incredibly foolish.

"Hey, Leo. I just came down to check on Tawny."

His mother stood in the doorway of the barn with a worried expression etched on her face. With her dark hair and soft brown eyes, she never seemed to age. It was surprising, considering what she'd been through in the last year and a half. Of all the members of the Duggan clan, it was Annie Mae Duggan who cared most for the horses at the ranch. She always said that she'd fallen in love with the horses well before she had been swept off her feet by Wesley Duggan.

"How's she doing?" Leo asked. Tawny was a well-loved gold and white mare who'd been under the weather for a few days now. They were all anxiously waiting for her to get better. Leo had gone down to the stables first thing this morning, but like his mother, he hadn't noticed any improvement in her condition.

She made a face. "She's a little more energetic today, but not eating much. I might have to reach out to Maya if we don't see some major improvement soon. It might be colic, but it could also be a virus. If that's the case, we need to keep her isolated from the rest of the horses. Ezekiel is going to keep a close eye on her as well. He's one of the most dependable ranch hands."

Leo hated to hear her confirm that things hadn't improved as much as they were all hoping. But he implicitly trusted his mother and their veterinarian, Maya Reynolds, who happened to be married to Ace. Between the two of them, he was certain they would get to the bottom of it.

"Let me know if you think we should make that call to Maya, Mama. Your judgment is always spot on."

His mother moved toward him and placed a kiss on his cheek. "Thanks for saying so. I feel like I'm finally coming out of the fog I've been in after losing your dad." She blinked back tears. "It hasn't been easy but focusing on the ranch and the horses has helped me immensely."

He ducked his head. "I understand. I'm still trying to work through it myself."

"You'll get there, son," she said, patting him on the back. "You and your dad were so close. I pray every day that you'll stop blaming yourself for his passing."

Me too, he wanted to say. He had never told his mother all the details regarding his absence from the ranch that day. She had no idea he'd left the Double D in order to meet up with Dahlia. Leo had paid for his girlfriend to fly to Owl Creek from Palmer so they could spend some time getting to know one another better in person rather than chatting online. Things had turned nightmarish when Dahlia stood him up and he'd returned to the ranch to a dying father.

Leo winced just recalling the details. Not only hadn't she shown up to see him, but she'd then broken up with him and completely disappeared from his life. It hadn't taken him long to figure out his feelings had never been reciprocated. Dahlia had never planned to come to Owl Creek. She had pocketed the money he'd sent instead of returning it. Falling in love with a coldhearted user had caused him a lot of heartache. And not being present while his father suffered a fatal seizure was something he would always bitterly regret. By training service dogs, he was hoping for a shot at redemption. It wouldn't bring his dad back, but it would help others who were at risk from serious medical conditions.

"I'm determined to honor him by helping others who could benefit from these services." Maybe it would help get him through the difficult mourning period he was still in the thick of.

"You're doing something really wonderful," his mother said. Emotion rippled in her voice. "Dad would be proud of your efforts."

Leo looked away from his mother as he tried to rein his emotions in. His throat felt clogged while his chest tightened. "I like hearing that," he admitted.

"Was that Kit O'Malley who just drove past me?" his mother asked. She couldn't hide her curiosity if she tried. Annie Mae wasn't a gossip, but she enjoyed being in the know.

"Yes, Mama," he said with a nod. "She just left here."

"What brought her way out to the ranch?" His mother's brows were knit together.

Leo wasn't sure how to answer the question. Kit hadn't yet told her parents about her medical condition, and he assumed they had no idea she was training with him and Jupiter. However, he knew his mother would be discreet.

"She's training with Jupiter," he admitted. "I can't give any details, but she's in need of a service dog."

She made a tutting sound. "I won't say a word, son. That poor girl has already suffered enough, what with raising a baby on her own and folks poking into her child's parentage. I'm wishing her the best. She'll be in my prayers."

Leo grinned down at his mother. "You're pretty wonderful. Do you know that?"

"Oh, you're making me feel all warm and fuzzy," she said, chuckling. "I'm going to head back to the house for lunch. Do you want to join me?"

"No, I'm going to wash up and then head into town to meet up with Ace. I don't get to see him much these days since he's running the Owl Creek dog shelter."

"That sounds fun. You need to spend more time away from the ranch," she said with an arched brow. "Send my love to Ace and Maya. And pick up one of Piper's pies," she called out as she sailed out of the barn with a wave of her hand.

By the time Leo made it into town, snowflakes were falling at a steady pace, making the downtown area resemble a picture-perfect Alaskan postcard. After parking his truck, Leo strolled down Main Street, pausing to speak to some of the townsfolk and to admire the festive shop windows. The diner was lit up with sparkly holiday lights and the sign flashed green and red in celebratory fashion. A festive wreath hung on the front door while several others adorned the windows.

The Snowy Owl Diner was a popular establishment in Owl Creek. Leo had happy childhood memories of eating breakfast there with his dad and Ethan. They'd always ordered blueberry flapjacks, rosemary-infused sausage and hot cocoa with plenty of marshmallows. Candy canes had always been handed out in abundance by the owner, Jack Miller. Piper—Jack's daughter—had inherited the place after his tragic death in a snowmobile accident. Piper, along with her now husband, Braden North, had also created a thriving side business, Pie in the Sky. Leo made a mental note to order a mixed berry pie to take back to the ranch for his mother.

"This place sure hasn't lost its charm," Leo said out loud as he admired the merry facade of the establishment. With all the wreaths and bows, it was bursting with holiday cheer.

Just as he reached the entrance, a petite figure draped in a dark cloak stumbled into him. He instinctively grabbed her by the elbow to prevent her from taking a tumble. The woman raised her head up in surprise and let out a startled sound. He found himself looking into Kit's green eyes. "L-Leo, I'm so sorry. I wasn't looking where I was going and it's a bit slippery."

"No worries," he said, letting go of her arm once he knew she was steady on her feet. He wondered if Kit's fading vision had anything to do with her near fall. Was she too proud to admit it? Pretty soon, they would be training Jupiter to aid Kit with her visual deficits. The dog would alert her to hazards in her path or any obstacles she couldn't see. For now, the goal was to have Jupiter work on the basics.

"This flurry of snow came out of nowhere," she said sheepishly, brushing snow off her hair. "I'm not even wearing a hat."

Leo reached out and opened the door, making a sweeping gesture with his hand. "After you," he murmured, stepping inside the restaurant once Kit entered. A sprig of mistletoe hung just inside the doorway. His parents had always shared a kiss in this very spot when they'd come to the diner. Each and every time, Leo had groaned with embarrassment. What he wouldn't give to see them smooch one more time. He might just give them a standing ovation.

A Christmas song blared from the jukebox, lending a lively air to the packed eatery. Kit began to hum along with the song, which was always the most requested song of the holiday season. Back when they were kids, she'd had the best voice in the church choir. Her sweet soprano voice had filled the rafters of the church with melodious sounds. The smell of food cooking on the griddle filled the space with mouthwatering aromas. Leo's stomach grumbled in response. It felt like ages since he had eaten breakfast.

"Are you meeting someone for lunch?" Leo asked, wondering if he should invite Kit to eat with him and Ace. It would be nice to spend some time with her outside of Jupiter's training.

"I'm just picking up some sandwiches for myself and Jules," Kit explained. "The shop got really busy with customers so she's holding down the fort while I pick up our order."

"I'm meeting up with Ace," he said, finding himself unable to tear his gaze away from her so he could look around the diner for his buddy. Every time he was in her presence, Leo's attraction toward her deepened. There had always been something so special about Kit. Her appeal had only grown over the years. Getting to know her better as adults was really nice.

"By the way, Leo, I've decided to sit down with my family in the next few days and tell them everything about my medical condition. And about training with Jupiter at the ranch." He sensed her nervousness about coming clean with her family, but he also detected fortitude. She'd clearly made up her mind and he believed she would follow through with her plans.

"I think that's wonderful," he said, reaching out and squeezing her hand. "Now you'll have their support and understanding. Keeping this huge secret must be stressful for you. You need allies." *Like me*, he wanted to add. He hoped Kit knew he was in her corner.

At that moment, Piper came rushing over toward them, greeting them with a vivacious smile and a cheerful greeting. "Hey there, guys. Long time no see, Leo. Follow me and I'll get you the best table in the house." With her curly brown hair and café au lait–colored skin, Piper was a charmer, one who had made her mark as a businesswoman in Owl Creek.

"Oh, Piper, we're not together," Kit blurted out, her cheeks flushing.

"I'm meeting Ace," he quickly explained, looking

around the diner until he spotted him sitting at a table toward the back. Was it his imagination, or was Piper looking at them as if they were a couple?

Kit pointed toward the pickup counter. "Jules called in an order for the two of us."

"Sorry about that," Piper said. "Come on over, Kit, and I'll check to see if it's ready."

Kit turned toward Leo and said, "Enjoy your lunch with Ace. I'll see you in a few days."

As she walked away, Leo's gaze trailed after her. *A few days.* It was a bit depressing that he wouldn't be training with her until Friday. He hadn't realized how much seeing her meant to him. Even though he had his family out at the ranch, loneliness still crept in from time to time.

Ace grinned up at him as Leo arrived at their table. Leo leaned down and clapped his best friend on the shoulder. Ace Reynolds was a former Iditarod racer who'd retired after a traumatic dog sled crash. He'd moved back to Owl Creek, accepted an offer to lead the Owl Creek Dog Rescue and married the woman of his dreams, Veterinarian Maya Roberts.

"How's it going?" Leo asked. "Married life seems to be treating you well." Ace appeared happy and relaxed, Leo noted. It was amazing how much things could change in a matter of months. Not too long ago, Ace had been jaded and defeated.

"I have no complaints," Ace said, leaning back in the booth and crossing his arms in front of him. Ace jerked his chin in Kit's direction. "You two look good together," his friend remarked as Leo sat down across from him.

"We're just friends. Nothing more," he explained. Now that Ace was happily settled down, he appeared to want the same domestic bliss for Leo. *Not happening*, he wanted to say.

Ace leaned in across the table. "But you could get out of the friend zone if you asked her out. Invite her to one of the holiday events in town. The spirit of the season is upon us."

Leo held up his hands. "I'm not looking for romance. You know that more than anyone." Almost against his will, Leo's gaze swung back toward Kit. She was talking in an animated manner to Piper, her head tilted back with laughter.

"I know you've been burned in the past, Leo, but you can't just hide away at the ranch for the rest of your life."

"I'm not hiding away," Leo protested. "I'm just keeping my head down and focusing on what truly matters—the Duggan ranch and my family's legacy. And my service dog training."

Ace shook his head. "Remember when we went to Bible class as kids and we learned about Noah and the Ark? The whole concept of being paired up two by two translates to humans as well." Ace tried to keep a straight face, but the corners of his mouth were twitching with merriment.

Leo burst out laughing along with his friend. Ace's sense of humor always made him crack up. "Noah's Ark, huh?"

Ace shrugged. "Whatever helps you see reason. If I remember correctly, you used to crush on Kit pretty fiercely back in the day."

He studied his menu, avoiding Ace's intense stare. "That was a long time ago. A lot has changed since then."

"What you're doing out at the ranch is amazing. Helping folks by pairing them up with service animals is a great way to honor your dad." Leo looked up and locked gazes with Ace. "Just make sure you stop to appreciate the world around you…and the people in it."

Leo let out a snort. "You're about as subtle as a sledgehammer."

Ace grunted. "I'm just hoping to get through to you. You're worthy of finding a good woman, Leo. Stop punishing yourself for the past."

Leo didn't have a snappy comeback to deliver.

As they both studied their menus, Leo's mind wandered to his conversation with Ace.

Was Ace right? Could he really live out a genuine love story with someone? Just the thought of being in a relationship made him feel squirmy and uncomfortable. He wasn't sure he could ever fully trust a romantic partner again.

How many times had he told himself that love had passed him by? He had convinced himself that he wasn't the settling down kind, even though it was all he'd ever wanted—a wife and kids. Kit's sweet face flashed before his eyes. It was stupid to wish for things with her that he didn't think would ever come to pass.

Despite the fact that he still had dreams of finding his other half, Leo knew he wasn't strong enough to endure another betrayal. Dahlia Reed had left too many scars in her wake. Because of her deception, she'd made him doubt his own judgment. His foolishness had led to him not being able to say goodbye to his father.

No way. Love was too much of a risk. He would be in the friend zone with Kit. And he would be supportive of all of her efforts to work with Jupiter. Anything else was out of the question.

Kit placed a closed sign on the front door of Second Time Around and turned the key to lock up the shop. The simple process was made difficult due to her trembling fingers. She pressed her eyes closed and began to pray to soothe her rattled soul.

"Everything's going to be all right. You'll be fine." No matter how many times Kit repeated the words out loud, she still didn't believe it. She was beginning to wonder if she wasn't the least fortunate person in all of Alaska. She had an appointment with a retinal specialist at the clinic, and Jules had promised to go with her. But a stomach bug had sidelined her sister late last night, and now she had to go by herself.

Kit hated the fact that she'd been relying so much on Jules to accompany her. Kit's independence was important to her, especially now, but seeing the eye specialist was nerve-racking. She'd counted on Jules to calm her down about meeting with Dr. Farrington.

"Locking up early?"

The deep voice came from over her shoulder, startling Kit. She quickly turned around, coming face-to-face with Leo. His gray winter hat and matching parka made him look rugged and stylish.

"Hey, Leo. How's it going?" Kit forced herself to smile as she greeted him.

"I'm fine. What's happening?" he asked, jerking his chin in the direction of the shop.

"I'm off to see the eye doctor. Dr. Farrington is a retinal specialist from Homer who comes over twice a month to see patients at the medical clinic."

Leo seemed to be studying her. "You don't look very happy about it."

"It's not that. Jules was supposed to come with me for moral support and now she's come down with a stomach virus." She was trying to swallow her disappointment, but it was difficult. She hated going to see Dr. Farrington all by herself. "So I'm closing up early so I can drive over to make my appointment."

"Do you want some company?" Leo asked. "I'm playing hooky today from work, so I've got nothing but time on my hands."

"What?" Kit asked. "No, I couldn't impose on you, Leo. You've already done so much for me by setting me up with a service animal and lessons."

"Kit, I can see you're nervous. And you're not asking. I'm offering."

Say yes, she told herself. *It's okay to lean on people.*

"Leo, I already feel indebted to you. How am I ever going to repay you for all of your kindnesses?"

"You can buy me a hot cocoa afterward and a chocolate chip cookie." He winked at her. "Those are my favorite. Come on," Leo coaxed. "Say yes."

"Yes," she said, offering him a grateful smile. "And thank you for offering. I can't explain why my nerves are so rattled about this appointment," she said, wrinkling her nose. "I hate feeling like this."

"It's understandable, especially if this is the doctor who gave you the bad news in the first place. Going back is bound to make you feel a bit antsy. That's why you shouldn't go alone."

Kit knew what Leo was telling her made total sense. A part of her worried she would get more bad news that she wouldn't be able to handle. Her main goal was to stay strong and positive for Ada. At moments like this, she was being tested.

"I appreciate it. The least I can do is drive us," Kit said as she led the way toward her truck she'd parked in front of the store.

"This is some ride," Leo said, letting out a low whistle. "This cherry red is such a great color. I've been admiring it for years."

"Thanks, it belonged to my dad who fixed it up and gave it to me as a birthday present," Kit said as she climbed up into the vehicle and sat behind the wheel. She turned toward Leo who was adjusting his seat belt on the passenger side. "I was sixteen when I started to drive. It gave me such a feeling of independence." She grinned, remembering how she had driven all over Owl Creek in celebration of getting her license. "Nothing could hold me back." She revved the truck and took off down Main Street. There was nothing as empowering as hitting the Alaskan roads. She considered it a major accomplishment to be able to navigate snow, freezing rain and ice.

Leo nodded. "Same here. My dad taught me how to drive out at the ranch. I remember that sensation of total freedom as I explored every inch of the property. There's nothing quite like it."

Kit agreed with him. It was one of those things most people took for granted. Like being able to walk or read a book. The very idea of not being able to drive filled her with an unbearable sadness.

"What if lose it? My sight? And my ability to drive," she blurted out. She didn't know what it was about Leo that made her so comfortable being open with him. He had a rare quality that most people didn't have. He was so solid and grounded. Maybe it would rub off on her. Right now, all her insecurities were on full display.

She could feel his gaze on her. "You'll cross that bridge when and if it happens. You really don't know if that will come to pass, so there's no point in making yourself miserable." Although Leo's voice was soothing, Kit continued to fret.

Kit was trying to think of calming thoughts, but the more she thought about losing a substantial amount of her vision, the greater her anxiety peaked. If only the doctor could tell her exactly how much of her vision would remain intact, then she would be in a better head space.

"Kit, are you all right? You're breathing kind of heavy."

"I—I'm just in my head about being visually impaired," she explained. She did feel jittery. Her pulse was racing, and her palms were moist.

"Kit, pull over for a minute," Leo instructed. "You need to be still for a little bit."

"We don't have time," she protested. "I'll be late." This wasn't an appointment she could afford to miss. Doctor Farrington was in high demand, and she was fortunate he'd traveled to Owl Creek to see patients.

"Pull over," Leo said in a firm voice that didn't allow for argument. Kit steered her truck to the side of the road, putting it in Park a few feet away from a cluster of Sitka trees.

Kit folded her arms across her chest. "Now what?" she asked, trying not to be aggravated at Leo. Maybe she should have made this trip to the clinic solo.

"Close your eyes," he instructed. "Now take a few deep breaths. Nice and easy." He began to breathe in and out. She did as he told her, focusing on the steady rise and fall of her chest.

Within a few minutes, she felt much better. Leo's technique had worked.

"I'm sorry for losing it. I promise you, I'm usually a lot stronger than this. Ever since I found out I have macular degeneration it feels like I'm falling apart," she confessed.

"I know it sounds like a cliché, but you're going to have to take this as it comes. You don't know for certain how much vision loss you'll suffer. That's why it's so important to keep these appointments and to make sure the lines of communication are open with your doctor."

"I'm trying," she said. "But my mind has a habit of taking me to the worst-case scenario."

Being in such close confines with Leo was a bit unnerving. His rugged energy filled the truck. "I know that I'm not in your shoes, but it seems to me that there's no point in thinking the worst before it happens. It's like waiting for a rainstorm and carrying around an umbrella every day.

"You're right. I know you are. It's just that ever since my diagnosis there's been this fear sitting in my gut. It's complicated because the only other time I've been afraid like this was when I found out I was pregnant." Kit looked away from Leo. She'd just opened up to him about something very personal that she didn't discuss with many people. It had taken months for Kit to recognize the baby she was carrying as a blessing. Before that moment, she'd lived with shame, regret and fear.

"Bringing a baby into the world on your own must've been overwhelming," Leo acknowledged. "I've always admired the way you held your head up high and carried on." He twisted his mouth. "I wish I'd told you so at the time."

She smiled at him. "It's great hearing it now. I think I'm ready to get back on the road."

"I think so too," Leo said, looking at his watch. "We're still making good time, so no speeding." The grin on his face told her he was teasing. Being in his presence had served the purpose of steadying her nerves. By the time they reached the clinic, most of Kit's anxiety was gone.

Leo didn't come inside the exam room with her but

remained in the waiting area. Right before she went in he flashed her a thumbs-up sign. It was such a small gesture, yet it gave Kit confidence. *You've got this,* she reminded herself. *You are a child of God—strong, smart, resilient. Beautifully made.*

After examining her at length, Dr. Farrrington said, "I can confirm my earlier diagnosis of macular degeneration. I don't see any evidence at the moment of disease progression. However, I'd like to give you some literature about different procedures that can slow its progression. Take some time to read it over and we can talk in a virtual appointment if you have any follow-up questions. We can also talk about the use of a cane as your eyesight worsens."

A cane! Kit had been thinking about acquiring one in order to keep herself steady as she walked. She looked forward to discussing it with the doctor.

"I appreciate it, Doc. I've started training with a service dog, and I'm really excited about working with him. It's given me a lot of hope."

"That's great, Kit. I've found that guide dogs become an integral part of my patients' adjustment to vision loss. There are many studies that demonstrate how service dogs improve every aspect of their owners' lives. Good for you for being so proactive!" He looked at his computer. "I'd like to see you next month."

"Sure thing," she said. "See you then." Kit went back to the waiting room where Leo was flipping through magazines to occupy himself. He stood up as soon as he spotted her.

"Everything okay?" he asked, his eyes full of questions.

She nodded. "Yes, everything went really well." Although her diagnosis hadn't changed, Doctor Farrington had presented options for treatment.

On the ride back to town, Kit filled Leo in on her appointment. He listened attentively and asked questions about next steps. *This man really knows how to be a good friend*, Kit realized. He'd gone above and beyond by accompanying her to this appointment and lifting her up.

Conversation flowed easily between them, and before she knew it, they were back on Main Street. Kit pulled up in front of Second Time Around and parked her truck.

"Leo, I truly can't thank you enough for coming with me today." Her words were inadequate to fully express her gratitude, but she wanted to try to let him know what it meant to her.

"It was my pleasure. All I did was come along for the ride," he said, shrugging.

"You did a lot more than that and you know it," Kit said. "Well, I'll see you Friday bright and early."

Leo let out a chuckle. "You're not getting off that easy, Miss O'Malley. I still want my hot cocoa." Leo smirked at her. "I've been thinking about it this whole time."

Somehow, she'd completely forgotten about their bargain. It was the least she could do after he'd shown her such grace and empathy.

"How about the North Star Chocolate Shop on Main

Street?" she asked. "They have these new chocolate chunk mint cookies that are amazing."

"I can't argue with perfection. You had me at North Star Chocolate."

"Okay then. Let's go." Kit grabbed her purse and stepped down from the truck. She walked over to the sidewalk and began heading toward the chocolate emporium with Leo by her side.

As they traveled down Main Street, Kit noticed curious glances in their direction. In a small town like Owl Creek, the residents always tried to pair people up. Little did they know that nothing romantic could never come to pass between her and Leo. Even their budding friendship was questionable. What would Leo say if he uncovered her secret? There was no doubt in her mind that he wouldn't want anything more to do with her. Their friendship would be severed, along with their working relationship. That knowledge served as a huge incentive to keep her secrets buried.

At the moment, she couldn't wrap her head around losing Leo's friendship. Or the chance to work with Jupiter.

Chapter Five

By the time Friday rolled around, Kit was itching to get back to the Duggan ranch and continue her training with Jupiter. It was funny how the sweet Labrador retriever had wiggled his way into her heart in such a short time. As she drove to the ranch, she thought about the fact that she hadn't yet told her parents anything about her condition. She had faltered at the last moment and the words hadn't come out.

It was silly to fret about it, but she worried what Leo would think of her lack of courage. She wasn't going to bring it up with him, but she suspected he might ask. Kit would be honest, but with so much on her plate, she refused to beat herself up about it. She would do it when the time was right.

When she drove up to the stables, Kit immediately noticed Leo was outside in the enclosure with Jupiter. Several ranch hands were scattered around the area. Some of the men were busy with a hay delivery, while others were tending to the horses. Kit parked her truck and immediately headed over in Leo's direction.

"Good morning, Kit," Leo said, moving toward the gate and opening it up for her.

"Morning," Kit answered as she stepped inside, admiring his powerful stride and the strong tilt of his head. Dressed in a dark pair of jeans, a black Stetson and a heavy corduroy jacket, Leo looked like the quintessential Alaskan cowboy.

Poor Jupiter was frantically wagging his tail and looking in her direction. She'd heard Leo give him the commands Heel and Stay, which the pup was managing to do beautifully. "He missed you," Leo remarked, looking back and forth between them.

"I missed him too," Kit admitted. "He's really grown on me."

"I thought we'd do part of our session outside today if that suits you. Fresh air and gorgeous views. Plus, we'll be out of the way of the delivery trucks."

"Sure," she said. "I've got my warmest coat and boots on, so I'm ready for anything." Over her last few visits, Kit had learned that the barn was a chilly place even with heaters. Once they began moving around, she didn't feel it so much, but by sheer virtue of living in Alaska, dressing warmly had been drilled into her head.

"Okay, call Jupiter over to you," Leo instructed. "He needs to know that you're who he's working for. Over the next few weeks, we're going to emphasize to Jupiter that you're his owner. Then we can actually train him to service your needs, present and future."

"Come," she said in a soft voice. Every time she instructed Jupiter, Kit felt like a fraud. What did she know about training a service animal? At the moment, Jupiter was staring at her with his big puppy dog eyes.

"You have to sound like you mean it," Leo advised, "otherwise he's not going to listen to your commands. He's picking up on your indecision."

She waited a few seconds and cleared her throat. "Come, Jupiter," Kit said in a firm voice, slapping her hand against her leg as she did so. Without hesitation, Jupiter ran toward her, stopping right in front of her and following her command to sit.

"That's how to do it. With conviction. Give him a reward for listening," Leo said, handing her a snack to give to Jupiter. The dog quickly devoured the treat while Kit lavished him with praise and patted the top of his head.

"Now he can run around for a bit. Let him get some of his energy out before we start working."

Kit giggled at the sight of Jupiter as he took off running. "He looks so happy." He was darting around in the snow, moving at a fast pace as he ran around the enclosed area.

"He's doing zoomies," Leo said, chuckling as his eyes followed after Jupiter. Kit could see how deeply Leo cared for his dogs.

"Zoomies?" Kit asked. She'd never heard the expression before, having never spent a lot of time around canines.

"It's when dogs run around in bursts of energy. Sometimes they make wild noises, but it's their way of expressing themselves. A lot of dog experts say it's a sign of happiness," Leo explained.

"I believe that," Kit said, smiling up at Leo. At the moment, she felt joyful too. It seemed that being with Leo and training with Jupiter made her feel more grounded and less fearful.

Their eyes held and locked. Leo quickly looked away, choosing instead to focus on Jupiter's antics. Was she making him uncomfortable?

"So, how did your family take the news about your condition?" Leo asked, staring out across the vast acreage that comprised Duggan ranch.

"I—I didn't tell them yet," she admitted, shifting uncomfortably from one foot to the other. Leo slowly turned his head to look at her. Her stomach sank at the stunned expression etched on his face.

A huff of air escaped his lips, and she could see the condensation forming from his breath and the cold December atmosphere.

"So what happened?" Leo asked, his brows knit together. "You seemed ready when we spoke at the Snowy Owl."

Kit shrugged and stuffed her mittened hands in her coat. "I lost my courage. It's hard to wrap my head around disappointing them again," she admitted, letting out a huge sigh.

"Why would you say that? You've done nothing wrong, Kit."

She blinked back tears. How could she explain to him the pain and worry she'd given her parents when she'd gotten pregnant by Ethan? She'd made things worse by refusing to name Ada's father. It had been a huge mess. Kit knew they loved their granddaughter with all their hearts, but it didn't change the circumstances surrounding her birth. Or their embarrassment when the whispers started as soon as she began to show. Just remembering those tension-filled days filled her with emotion. The idea of falling apart in front of Leo made her feel weak. She wanted to show him that she was strong. "I'm the daughter who brought a child into the world without the benefit of marriage. Owl Creek is a wonderful community, but not everyone has been kind. I know my parents felt let down by me." Tears slid down her face.

Leo reached out and wiped her tears away with his thumb. "Your parents love you. They can be disappointed by certain things, but at the same time still love and support you. And you need them right now to stand by you and Ada."

"I know that they'll be there for me, just as they were when Ada was born." Memories of her parents fussing over their newly born grandchild came into sharp focus. "Maybe it's more about my pride than anything else. For so many years, I tried to be perfect. God sure has a funny way of showing me I'm not," she said with a brittle laugh.

"God doesn't make mistakes, Kit. So not only does that apply to the birth of your daughter, but to you as well. He loves you, flaws and all."

Kit had been questioning God so much as of late. Why her? At times, it had felt as if He had forsaken her. Why had He placed so many challenges in her path? Leo's words were encouraging. He was right about Adaline. Her daughter was a blessing. A verse from Psalms washed over her. *Lo, children are an heritage of the Lord: and the fruit of the womb is his reward.*

Adaline was a precious gift, despite the circumstances of her birth. Kit had always known this was true and clearly Leo believed it as well.

"I like that you're a man of faith," Kit said. "I'm a believer too, even though I've been asking the Lord a lot of questions in the past few weeks."

Leo shook his head. "Nothing wrong with that. I still ask Him why he took both Ethan and my dad." He made a face. "I don't have any answers yet, but I'm still being prayerful about it."

Jupiter ran over and stood right in front of them with an expectant look on his face.

"I think he's ready for us," Kit said with a chuckle. Jupiter's energetic personality served as a healing balm for Kit. Being around him made her spirit soar.

Leo nodded and said, "I think you're right. Show us what you've got, Jupe."

For a moment, Kit just stood and breathed in air. She was exactly where she needed to be at the moment—working with Leo and her new service dog. Kit knew she would need her faith to sustain her in the weeks and months to come. She had made the follow-up appointment with Dr. Farrington to discuss possible treatments. Although a cure was out of the question, the brochures she'd been given indicated the existence of several treatments that might slow the progression of her condition. It was nerve-racking just thinking about it, but as Leo said, she had to be hopeful.

Lord, please let there be something positive looming on the horizon. Please keep listening to my prayers.

As far as December in Alaska went, today's weather forecast was defying all logic as well as the *Farmers' Almanac*. According to the weatherman, the temperature was going to climb to a balmy fifty degrees, which was unusual in Owl Creek. There was a zero percent chance of snow, which made Leo shake his head. Snow was a daily occurrence in December, even if it was merely a few snowflakes dusting the ground. Perhaps this was his father's doing, he thought with a smile. Was he up in Heaven pulling some strings so the anniversary of his death would be a beautiful day?

Leo had known this day was coming, but it had crept up on him. He hadn't been fully prepared for the emotional aspects of this somber anniversary. First thing this morning, he'd ridden across the property with his mother and his dad's brothers, Uncle Patrick and Uncle Jamie. He'd tried to keep busy with work at the ranch, but thoughts of his father kept intruding on his thoughts. Had it really been a year since they'd lost him? Since he'd spoken to him? Asked him for advice? Seen him dancing cheek to cheek under the moon with his mother? All he had now were memories. They would have to sustain him for the rest of his days.

He and Kit had arranged for a later session this afternoon due to her busy schedule at the shop. Leo went through the training on autopilot. His thoughts kept wandering to the tragic day one year ago when he'd returned to the ranch to find his father dying. He couldn't manage to focus, which wasn't fair to Kit. She needed to get as much training under her belt as possible before her disease progressed.

Once the training session was finished, Leo and Jupiter walked Kit outside. If he were being completely honest with himself, he was a little bit off his game today. He was ending the session a tad early and it didn't feel right to shortchange Kit. The stakes were high for her. She would greatly benefit from having a guide dog in the near future.

"Sorry to end early today," he said by way of an apology. "We've got a lot going on here at the ranch." His ran a weary hand over his jaw. "One of our horses is doing poorly. Maya's going to come out to take a look at her so we'll know if it's anything serious or not. We did a virtual appointment with her and now she wants to come out in person."

Kit's eyes widened and she let out a fretful sound. "Oh, no. I hope everything turns out all right." She reached out and touched his arm, creating an awareness of her that he'd been trying to stuff down. "If anyone can help, it's Maya. She's a fantastic veterinarian."

"She is," he said with a nod. "Owl Creek is fortunate to have her. A lot of small towns in Alaska don't have access to care for large animals."

"That's a good point," Kit said with a shake of her head. "She's going to be Jupiter's vet when he comes to live with me." A contented look was etched on her face. "I have full confidence in Maya's abilities."

Leo stopped in his tracks just as he reached the fenced area leading to the pasture. At the crack of dawn, he'd watched as his mother placed his father's favorite flowers a few feet away from where Leo was standing now in a place that had been meaningful to Wesley Duggan. A pale yellow ribbon for remembrance bound up the forget-me-nots. The bright blue flowers were the official state flower of Alaska. It was yet another reminder of all they'd lost. His mother's intentions had been heartfelt, but seeing the blooms caused an ache in his heart.

"That bouquet is beautiful. I love forget-me-knots," Kit said, pausing to admire the display.

"They're for my dad. My mother placed them there. Today is the anniversary of his death," Leo explained. His emotions were in overdrive today. He was a bit surprised he'd been able to get the words out of his mouth. What was it about Kit that made her so easy to talk to?

Kit swung her gaze toward him. "Oh, Leo. I'm so sorry. I know this must be such a tough day for you. You could have rescheduled our training if you needed a day off. I would have understood." Her tone was soft and laced with compassion.

He looked down and dragged his booted foot through the snow. "Thanks, Kit, but I wanted to try and make it a normal day." He shrugged. "Or as normal as possible under the circumstances. Also, it wouldn't be fair to you. Jupiter is doing well, but there's a huge amount of training in both of your futures. We have so much ground to cover."

"I get it," she said, reaching down to pat Jupiter,

"You're going to mourn his loss for the rest of your life. It'll ease up little by little. Just make sure you take the time to celebrate him today."

Celebrate? He hadn't really thought of the sad anniversary in those terms. Leo was still so knee-deep in mourning that he found it difficult to view this day in any way other than one steeped in sorrow.

"My grandmother died in an accident when I was twelve. Every year we buy balloons and release them at the cemetery on the day she passed. We go around and share something wonderful about her." Kit gifted him with a beautiful smile. "It's our way of honoring her on a day that brought us so much sadness. It kind of flips it around so it's not all sadness. I guess you can call it a tribute."

Leo would do anything to turn a page on his grief. There were so many wonderful things about his father that Leo had pushed out of his mind in order to spare himself pain. But wasn't it worse to stuff it all down and not rejoice in his life? By not talking about him, wasn't he simply erasing him? Perhaps it was the guilt he was still clinging to. Leo suspected it was still holding him back from facing his father's death in a healthy way. But how could he let go of the shame and culpability?

Kit's take on the situation was spot on. She'd just exposed one of his huge weaknesses and shone a light on it. Just as Kit was learning from him about service dogs, Leo was acquiring knowledge from his student. Her heartfelt words resonated with him more than he'd ever imagined.

"You're right," he acknowledged. "I've been so wrapped up in mourning him that I've forgotten to honor his life." He shoved a hand through his hair. "Makes me feel kind of foolish. Yet again I've dropped the ball."

"Leo!" Kit's eyes flashed with a hint of anger. "Stop beating yourself up about it. Didn't you tell me that training service dogs was your way of honoring your father?"

"It is," he said. It was his penance as well for forsaking his father for a fake online profile and the lure of romance. Leo hoped one day he could forgive himself.

"He'd be so proud of you for helping people like me. I imagine your mom is too."

"He was always proud of me," Leo said. "Ethan was the war hero, but my father thought the sun rose and set on me." Leo had loved Ethan dearly, but he'd often felt as if he had lived in his cousin's shadow. There hadn't been a single thing Ethan hadn't excelled at. He had always been honored to be Ethan's cousin, but making his own path in Owl Creek had been challenging.

A trace of a smile twitched at the corners of her mouth. "You were a very well-behaved child from what I remember." She tapped her finger against her chin. "Although there was that incident with the possum."

Leo raised his hands up in the air and chuckled. "That was not me! Honestly. I was just in the wrong place at the wrong time. Hanging around with Ace and the North brothers always got me in trouble."

Kit's shoulders shook with laughter. "That was quite a crew. Always up to mischief."

"I'm so thankful for having grown up in a tight-knit

community like Owl Creek. The town is planning to recognize Ethan for his military service during the holiday stroll. I figured it would bring back the pain of losing him, but I've been wrong in my thinking. It's a way for Aunt Ivy and Uncle Jamie to see him celebrated."

A surprised expression passed over her face. "I—I think that would be wonderful for your family. Ethan was a town hero."

Just hearing someone else say it out loud caused a warm feeling to spread across his chest. Regardless of often feeling second best in comparison to his cousin, he'd always adored Ethan, and they'd shared a close bond. "He was. And his sacrifice should be recognized. It'll mean a lot to all of us Duggans," Leo said. "Is your shop a part of the festivities?"

"Yes, we're going to have a street sale and hang up all the items outside and make it really festive with red and green balloons, candy canes and lots of tinsel."

Leo couldn't help but notice how her eyes twinkled with excitement as she spoke.

"That sounds great. It's obvious how much you're enjoying owning a business. That's how I feel about working on the ranch."

"I'm really passionate about vintage pieces, especially clothes," Kit explained. "I get a huge thrill out of discovering these items and then reselling them. It's like taking a walk through the past." She took a quick look at her watch. "Oops. I've got to scoot and get back into town. Thanks for the lesson, Leo."

"I'm grateful for your words of encouragement. They've given me a new perspective." He looked around at the ranch's vast acreage. "He's here, Kit. My dad is all around me, especially at the Double D. He loved this ranch more than anything else in creation. That's a huge part of his legacy." Leo felt his chest easing up a bit. All this emotion had been bottled up inside him. It was a relief to get it out.

It still hurt to have lost him, but he needed to talk about his father. Who he was as a man of faith. The activities he'd enjoyed. The funny dad jokes he'd shared with him and his younger sister, Tiffany.

"I'm happy to have helped," Kit said, bending down and scratching the area behind Jupiter's ears. "See you next time, big boy." Leo watched as she drove off down the road and away from him. Leo got down on his haunches so he was eye-level with Jupiter.

"She's super nice, isn't she? And easy on the eyes." Jupiter responded by licking the side of Leo's face. Leo chuckled at Jupiter's exuberance. "Okay, boy. That's enough. You did a decent job today, but you can't get distracted. Pretty soon we're going to be taking you out to public places. You've got to focus a little bit more."

The crunch of tires on the road interrupted the moment, bringing attention to the sheriff's vehicle pulling into the driveway. Leo raised his hand in greeting as Sheriff Hank Crawford stepped out of the car. Hank was an old friend of his. Hank's sister, Piper, ran the Snowy Owl Diner. In a small town like Owl Creek everyone was acquainted with one another. As a result, he and Hank had been connected for most of their lives. Hank was married to Sage, who was the granddaughter of Beulah North, the town matriarch.

"Hey there, Leo," Hank said as he strode toward him. "It's good to see you."

"Hi, Hank. Likewise," Leo said. "Trudy told me you're picking up Artemis for her."

Hank's mother, Trudy, was an insulin-dependent diabetic. He'd trained her to work with Artemis, another pup from Daisy's litter. Having graduated from the program, Artemis was ready to go home to Trudy, who wasn't able to make it out to the ranch today due to greeting guests at her bed-and-breakfast.

"Yeah, she can't wait to have him home with her. I want to thank you, Leo, for working to pair her up with Artemis. It's going to be awesome for her to have a service dog to help her out."

"They're a great team. Trudy and Artemis did all the work."

"Beulah wanted me to run something by you," Hank said. "She's in charge of the holiday stroll this year and she's incorporating some of Ace and Maya's rescue pups into the celebration. She wants to include your service dogs as well."

"What would we be doing?" Leo asked. The dogs were all trained to be out in public with the exception of Jupiter.

"From the sounds of it, your group would be walking around with the service pups. She figures it would be a great way to shine a light on your program and showcase the dogs and their owners." Hank grinned. "And who doesn't love dogs?"

Leo had yet to meet anyone who disliked dogs. They were man's best friend after all. Lovable and likeable.

"Hmm. I like the sounds of it," Leo said. "All of the participants spent countless hours training with the dogs. This could be a fun way to celebrate all their hard work."

"So you're in?" Hank asked. "Beulah can be pretty persuasive, so she might give you a call to seal the deal."

Leo chuckled. He, along with the rest of the town, knew all too well that Beulah North was a woman who was a force to be reckoned with. "Let me reach out to everyone and get their opinion. I'll circle back to you, if that's okay."

"It's fine by me," Hank said. "Not sure if Beulah will be okay with it," he teased.

"I guess it's time for me to hand over Artemis," Leo said, wishing he didn't have a tugging sensation in the region of his heart.

A few minutes later, Artemis was sitting in the sheriff's vehicle with Hank. The Labrador had his head stuck out the window as they drove away. Leo tore his gaze away from them, not wanting to be a glutton for punishment.

It hadn't been easy handing over his pups to all their new owners. He'd become accustomed to taking care of them and forging a bond with each one. Although he knew they would now be working for a greater good, it still caused a little hitch in his heart every time he said goodbye. They were all such great pups.

Just at that moment, Daisy came trotting toward him, trailed by Jupiter. The sight of the two dogs lifted his spirits. Well, at least he still had two dogs left. *But not for long*, he thought. Jupiter was going through his training like a champ. It was working out way better than he'd imagined. He couldn't be more thrilled for Kit. She was a good woman who deserved to live out the rest of her life happy and content. Jupiter would keep her safe.

Kit's happiness mattered to him way more than he wanted to admit to himself. He pushed the thought away, knowing it wasn't the right time to examine those emotions. For the remainder of the day, he planned to do everything in his power to celebrate his father.

Chapter Six

Kit left the Double D Ranch with a gnawing feeling in her gut. She'd somehow managed to hold it together when Leo mentioned the fact that Ethan was being honored at the holiday stroll. In reality, the news had made her feel like an imposter. How dare she accept Leo's time and generosity while sitting on this powder keg about Ethan? If Leo had any inkling about the secret she was hiding, he wouldn't want anything to do with her.

Adaline's father was a town hero. He had lost his life serving in the United States military. And yet, if she continued on this path, her daughter would never know that her father was a beloved figure in Owl Creek. No matter how Kit tried to justify withholding the truth, it just didn't feel right anymore. Spending time with Leo was making her dilemma even more tension-filled. He'd loved his cousin and still deeply mourned him.

Leo was a good man who was going to great lengths to help her. Her conversation with him had given her

the strength to be open and honest with her parents. If
Leo could face his grief on the anniversary of his father's passing, Kit could find the resolve to be frank
and honest with her family about her macular degeneration diagnosis. It was high time she fessed up. Seamus and Rose O'Malley were gentle and hardworking
people who cared deeply for their three children. The
thought of wounding them with the news of her medical
condition was causing her a lot of angst. This time of
year was supposed to be merry and bright. Celebratory.
So far it had been fraught with uncertainty and anxiety.

Hope is a part of the Christmas season, she reminded
herself. It hung in the very air this time of year. She had
to try to stay as positive as possible if she was going to
make it through this raging storm. When Kit finished
setting up for the holiday sale at Second Time Around,
it was closing time.

She'd intended to go through with telling her parents
about her diagnosis, but her nerves were too frazzled by
the time everyone sat down at the dinner table. Placing
Adaline in her high chair put everything in perspective.
Every step she took was for her little girl. Nothing mattered more to Kit than her happiness and prosperity.

Knowing Leo had her back gave her a huge boost.
He exuded such strength and decency. It made her feel
all the more ashamed that she hadn't been honest with
his family about Adaline. Her stomach twisted at the
mere idea of Leo ever finding out the truth. It hurt to
know he might think poorly of her. His good opinion
meant a lot to her. Knowing he'd bent over backward
to come up with a way to include her in his service

animal training made her feel special. She hadn't felt that way in a long time.

Leo was such a good man, and she was beginning to lean on him as her service dog trainer. His patience and wisdom were endless. She wondered what it would be like to have a man like Leo by her side. Kit imagined he would be loving and kind. He put others first and didn't have a mean bone in his body. When they were kids, he had always taken on the schoolyard bullies to protect the weaker students. Although she felt guilty thinking it, Leo was pretty swoon-worthy.

Stop romanticizing him! she chided herself. Leo was completely off-limits to her based on her past history with Ethan. It didn't matter if he was wonderful or not. The secret that stood between them would doom any potential relationship. Not that Leo had done anything to indicate a romantic interest in her. He'd been nothing but professional at all times. She needed to get herself together and focus on the matter at hand.

Kit pushed her food around her plate, too nervous to eat much of the meal. Jules looked at her from across the table, urging her with eye movements to open up a dialogue with their family. Knowing her sister, she might just cut to the chase and deliver the news on Kit's behalf.

"I need to tell you all something." Kit blurted the words before she chickened out. A heavy weight was sitting on her chest. She figured if nothing else, it would be a huge relief to confide in her loved ones.

"What is it?" her younger brother Tad asked. "Did you buy me an early Christmas gift?"

Everyone laughed, knowing the eleven-year old was fond of having gifts bestowed on him, whether it was the holiday season or not. The merriment helped ease some of the tension that had built up inside her. She wasn't trembling as much as she had been a few moments ago.

Kit reached over and held on to her mother's hand as she spoke. "This isn't going to be easy for you to hear, but I've been diagnosed with macular degeneration."

Her mother let out a gasp, while her father groaned and covered his face with his hands.

"Oh, no," Seamus cried out. "I always feared this might happen because of your grandfather." James O'Malley had been diagnosed before her dad had been born. Seamus had been well aware of his dad's disability for his entire life. He's seen his father struggle both in his personal life and professionally as a result of his disability.

"What's going on?" Tad asked. Her brother had no clue about macular regeneration and what it meant for Kit's life. Jules leaned over and placed her arm around Tad.

"It means that Kit's vision is going to be fading over the next few weeks and months. The whole process could take years," Jules said in a gentle tone. "We'll have to be extra helpful to assist her and Ada."

Tad swiveled his head so his gaze was focused on Kit. "Are you going to be blind?" he asked with wide eyes. It was the same query that kept Kit up at night, tossing and turning. The very thought of it was terrifying, but she knew it was a distinct possibility.

She swallowed past the bile rising up in her throat. "Honestly, I don't know. I may not lose all of my sight, but it's going to progress to a point where driving and other things will be out of the question. I'm already experiencing vision loss and most likely it will continue to worsen. Remember the bad fall I took? That was due to my eyesight. My life is going to be very different, Tad, and I'm going to face a lot of challenges."

Kit's father began to openly sob. "I feel like this is all my fault. I'd rather this be happening to me than you, Kit."

Kit stood up from her chair and quickly reached her father's side. She wrapped her arms around him and tightly hugged him. His whiskers grazed her cheek pressed against his. "Please don't blame yourself. We've always known this was lurking in our DNA. It's nobody's fault."

"You're one of the strongest people I know," her mother said, dabbing at her eyes with a napkin. "We'll do everything in our power to support you. I promise we won't let you down."

All the while, Ada continued to eat her meal, seemingly unperturbed by the drama unfolding before her eyes. She was making smacking noses and enjoying her food. Kit was thankful for small blessings. In Ada's little world, nothing was amiss. Kit would love to keep it that way for as long as she could.

"It's not all doom and gloom," Kit said, forcing herself to sound chipper. "There may be some promising treatments to slow the disease's progression and I'm training my very own service dog with Leo Duggan out at the Double D Ranch." She turned toward Tad. "My dog is named Jupiter, and he's a Labrador retriever. You're going to love him as much as I do."

Tad let out a squeal of joy. "Really? We're getting a dog?"

His exuberance brought a smile to her face. "Well, he'll be my service dog, so there are some rules you'll have to follow, but he'll be one of the family. Jupiter loves rubs and treats. His main job is to help me with tasks and keep me safe."

"That's so cool," Tad raved. "I can't wait to meet him. He sounds really smart."

"Oh, he is," Kit said, winking at her brother.

"We know this is extremely hard to endure, Kit," Jules said, "but we believe in you. We've got your back."

Kit felt comforted by her family's support and words of encouragement. She was discovering with each day that she was stronger than she'd realized. And even though she felt alone at times, it was the furthest thing from the truth. God was always with her, shining His light upon her. And her family would never allow her to fall.

It was strange, but all she wanted to do was drive over to the Duggan ranch and share her news with Leo. Kit knew he would be thrilled that she'd finally spoken to her family and gotten their support. She shook off the impulse. There was no point in getting overly attached to him. Leo was an old friend who she'd begun to rely on more than anyone else as of late. When their training ended, they would both continue separately with their lives, although Kit's world would be altered immeasurably by her condition. There wouldn't be anything else joining them together. That reality made her heart sink.

Maybe she should tell Leo the truth about Adaline. Perhaps it wouldn't be as bad as she was imagining. She'd summoned the courage to tell her parents the truth about her medical condition and the world hadn't stopped revolving on its axis. Was God trying to tell her something? One of her favorite Bible verses from John came to mind. *God is a Spirit: and they that worship him must worship him in spirit and in truth.*

Truth went hand in hand with her faith. The time had come to step up and live in her truth.

Chapter Seven

❧

"I think it's safe to say Tawny has colic," Maya Reynolds announced as she finished examining the sickly mare. "She's exhibiting all the classic symptoms. Pain in her abdomen. A decrease in appetite. An increase in her breathing."

Leo let out the tightly held breath he'd been keeping. Although he knew colic was a serious condition, he was also aware of the high survival rate with immediate treatment. There had been several horses at the ranch over the years who'd suffered from the condition.

"Colic responds well to treatment in the majority of horses," Maya explained. "I'm going to get her started on medication right away. I'll be checking in tomorrow to see if there's any change."

"Poor baby," his mother said, nuzzling the mare's face with her knuckles.

"I don't think she's going to need surgery, Annie. Colic can be complicated and painful, but I don't think this is a severe case," Maya explained.

"Praise the Lord," Annie said, looking over at Leo with tears pooling in her eyes.

Leo knew his mother's affection for this particular horse was tied up in the fact that his father had hand-picked Tawny at a horse auction in Fairbanks. He'd named the horse himself and lavished her with affection. Tawny was a direct link to her beloved husband.

His mother was such a loving woman. He valued her all the more due to the fact that two close members of his family were no longer with them. Nothing mattered more to him than family. Despite the challenges of being in mourning, Leo intended to do everything in his power to make this Christmas heartwarming and joyful.

Leo reached out and squeezed his mother's hand. Her emotions were palpable.

"Thanks for coming out here, Maya. We'll make sure to keep you posted on Tawny's progress," Leo said.

Maya dug around in her bag and pulled out a packet, which she handed to Leo. "This will get Tawny started until you can pick up the prescription at the clinic. It was nice seeing both of you. I'm sure we'll run into each other at the holiday stroll." She leaned in and hugged Annie. "I'm so glad Owl Creek is honoring Ethan this year."

"It means a lot to us, especially coming from within our community," Leo said. Owl Creek was all he'd ever known. He had the feeling not all towns were so giving and tight-knit.

"Despite our losses, we consider ourselves blessed,"

Annie said with a smile. It was wonderful to see his mother so grounded in her gratitude.

"Amen," Leo said. "Especially during the most special time of the year." Little by little, he was getting more excited about the holidays. He'd been eyeing a train set for Florence's twins that he needed to purchase at the toy store before it sold out. Experiencing the joy of Christmas morning through their eyes would be such a treat and a throwback to the ones he'd shared with Ethan. His own sister was ten years younger than Leo, so they'd always been at different stages in life, whereas Leo and Ethan had been contemporaries. So many memories pressed against Leo's heart. Between his mother and Kit, Leo was being reminded that instead of viewing them through a lens of sorrow, he needed to be thankful.

"Let me walk you outside, Maya," his mother suggested. "Leo, I'm heading back to the house, so I'll see you later." She looped her arm through Maya's and led her outside.

A few minutes later, Leo administered Tawny's first dose of the medicine. He was praying it made a difference. "There you go, girl. Hopefully you'll start to feel better soon." Leo hated witnessing any animal in pain. As a kid, he'd wanted to rescue every broken-winged bird he came across.

Leo left the stables and set about fixing a few breaks in the fencing around the property. The last thing they needed was for one of the livestock to end up missing from the pasture. As he rode across the property, Leo took a moment to soak in the landscape. Because of the hard work of his family, the Duggan ranch would serve as an enduring legacy. After finishing up his work, Leo headed back toward the outbuildings. He dismounted his horse, took off his saddle and then led him into the stables to cool down. The sight of a familiar-looking truck coming down the road halted him in his tracks. A few minutes later, Kit emerged from the vehicle with Adaline by her side. For a moment, he was totally confused. They weren't scheduled for a training session until tomorrow.

Leo called out to her. "Hey there, Kit. What brings you out here?" His pulse began to race a bit. The only occasions she'd ventured to the ranch had been related to her desire to train with a service dog. He hoped nothing was wrong.

As she walked toward him, Leo took a moment to admire her. In her pink-colored parka and dark corduroy pants, she looked really nice.

"Hi, Leo." She placed Ada on the ground. "Say hello to Leo, Adaline."

Adaline looked up at him and gave him a little wave with her chubby fingers.

"When I was here yesterday, I left my satchel. It holds my key to the shop," Kit explained. "These days I feel as if I'd forget my head if it weren't attached."

"You've got a lot on your plate," Leo answered. He wished that Kit could give herself more credit. She was juggling so many things while dealing with a dire medical diagnosis and taking care of Adaline.

"Why didn't you call me? I would have been happy

to drop the bag off at the shop and save you a trip out here." Lately, he'd been venturing into town more often, eager to come out of his self-imposed cocoon.

"I didn't want to be a bother," Kit admitted. A sheepish expression crossed over her face.

"That's not possible," he said, locking eyes with her. Something flickered in the air between them. An awareness of one another that hummed and crackled between them. Kit appeared startled by it. Just then Adaline tugged at her hand and pointed toward the pasture. "Horseys, Mama."

Kit broke eye contact with Leo and looked down at her daughter. "Yes, sweetheart. Lots of beautiful horseys." She looked up at Leo, chuckling. "Horseys sounds so much better than horses, doesn't it?"

Leo laughed along with her and nodded. "You're right about that."

"Okay, I'm going to try and locate my satchel. I have to get back to town and pick up some groceries," Kit said. "Ada, come with Mama."

"Why don't I help you look for the bag," Leo offered. "Between the two of us, we'll find it."

"Another pair of eyes would be great," Kit said, taking Adaline by the hand and heading toward the barn. Adaline let out a cry as she spotted Rufus the rooster strutting around.

A few minutes later, Kit let out a triumphant sound. "Found it. Yay!" she said, holding the dark brown satchel up in the air. Adaline began clapping and saying, "Yay," over and over again.

She was a sweet little girl, Leo realized. And she thought Kit hung the moon. Their relationship was very endearing. Kit exhibited all the qualities of being a loving and engaged mother.

"Okay, I'm going to run, Leo," Kit said, intruding on his thoughts. "Thanks for helping in the search for my satchel."

"It was my pleasure. Bye, ladies," Leo said, waving at them. "See you soon."

"Bye," Adaline chirped. Leo wanted to give the little tyke a hug goodbye, but she still hadn't completely warmed up to him. It was understandable. At six feet tall, he probably resembled a giant to her. All she knew was that he was mommy's friend, one who popped up from time to time. Watching the deep connection between mother and daughter was heartwarming. It made him think about things he'd thought were in his rearview mirror, such as having his own children and teaching them how to ride a horse.

But a big part of him still resisted the idea of allowing a woman too close to his heart.

He couldn't imagine being that vulnerable ever again.

A few moments later, the creaking sound of the barn door caused him to turn around.

Kit stood in the doorway with Ada in her arms. Her cheeks were rosy from the cold. A strange expression was stamped on her face.

"Back so soon?" Leo asked. "I thought you'd already left. Don't tell me you forgot something again," he teased. He wasn't complaining. Every time she appeared, Leo's pulse skittered and a warm feeling spread around his chest.

Kit shook her head, brown tendrils swirling around her face. "No, I didn't. But you're stuck with us for a little while longer, Leo. My truck just died on me."

So much for her telling Leo that Ethan was Adaline's father! Her best intentions from last night had fizzled out like a popped balloon. Being near to Leo was a bit disconcerting, especially when they were standing so close that Kit could smell his woodsy scent and see the flecks in his hazel eyes. It shouldn't have surprised her that she was acutely aware of him. After all, it had always been Leo she had been crushing on in her teen years. Not Ethan. What would Leo think if he knew the truth about her and his cousin? She wasn't about to tell him and run the risk of him pulling her out of the service dog program. It was selfish of her, but she needed Jupiter.

And now she was worried about her truck and getting Adaline back home. Driving was getting more difficult, especially when it got dark.

At the moment, Leo was sitting behind the wheel of her vehicle, trying to start it for the tenth time to no avail. After attempting once more to jump start it with Ezekiel's help, Leo stepped out of the truck. Ezekiel shook his head, indicating it was a lost cause.

Leo looked in Kit's direction. "I think we're going to have to call an auto repair shop."

Kit let out a groan. The truck had been acting up lately, but she hadn't had the time to take it into the shop. She should have known better. "Oh, no. That's a shame." She bit her lip. Having to pay for auto repairs right before Christmas would be tough on her wallet. "I always use Freddy's Auto Repairs. His prices are really affordable."

"Let me call over there so they can send someone out here," Leo said, reaching into his jacket pocket and pulling out his cell phone.

"I appreciate it," she said, wrapping a blanket around Adaline and handing her a bottle. The milk was no longer warm, but Adaline didn't seem to care as she thirstily drank from it.

"Kit, I'm going to drive you over to the house where you'll be nice and toasty. It's going to take a while before Freddy can get here to take a look at your truck."

"Oh no, I wouldn't dream of intruding on your family." The last thing she wanted to do was come face-to-face with the Duggan clan, particularly Ethan's parents. She'd managed to avoid them since she gave birth to Ada. Kit wasn't sure she could even look them in the eye at this point, knowing that she was hiding their granddaughter's existence from them.

Leo narrowed his gaze as he stared at her. "Come on, Kit. The temperature will be dipping drastically in a little bit. Think of Adaline. You don't want her to get sick."

Leo was right. It was already frigid out here. She couldn't expose her child to such low temperatures! And it was going to be getting dark soon, which worried her. Kit's night vision was not the best, especially now.

She bobbed her head. "You're right," she agreed,

reaching down to take her daughter's hand in her own. "Thanks for opening your home to us."

"Of course," he said, leading the way toward his truck. "Let me go get Ada's car seat and I'll put it in my truck." Leo quickly made the transfer and had no problem installing the car seat. "Don't worry. I'm a pro at this due to Florence's twins," he said.

Kit wasn't worried at all. Leo always exuded an air of stability. She trusted him implicitly.

Being invited to the Duggans' home felt a bit surreal. How many times over the past year had she wanted to reach out to Ethan's family and tell them about Ada? Each time she'd chickened out, just as she had earlier with Leo. If only she could be certain it wouldn't create a firestorm around Adaline. Her number one job in this world was to protect her daughter at all costs. She couldn't bear the thought of her being in a tug-of-war between her and the Duggans.

On the ride over to the house, Kit tried to quell her nerves as she gazed out the window. What if they took one look at Adaline and saw Ethan imprinted all over her darling little face? She had inherited his stunning blue eyes and perfectly shaped nose. She began breathing heavier than normal as her panic rose. What would she do if one of the family made the connection between Ethan and Adaline?

Leo looked over at her. "Are you all right? You're awfully quiet. I promise my family won't bite."

"I—I'm fine. Just taking in the view. It's spectacular." And it truly was magnificent.

A huge expanse of acreage stretched out before her.

Horses and cows dotted the snowy landscape. A large multilevel home rose up to greet them a quarter of a mile down the road. She let out a sigh at the sight of the amazing house. The front door was adorned with a large wreath with gold ribbons attached to it. Red and white candy canes decorated the path leading to the large wraparound porch. She knew it must look spectacular at night with all the Christmas lights blazing.

Leo pulled into a pebbled driveway and put the truck in Park. He turned toward her and said, "Quite a few of us live out here at the ranch. You've probably seen them all in passing over the years. And I know you and Florence are old friends."

She bobbed her head but didn't speak. Her pulse was racing wildly. It was too late to turn back now, she realized. She just needed to push past her nervousness and put on a brave face. There was no way in the world they would ever suspect Adaline was Ethan's daughter. It was simply her guilt working overtime and making her feel paranoid.

No sooner had they exited the car when Kit heard the sound of footsteps crunching on the snow. A petite woman with auburn hair streaked with gray came rushing down the steps toward them. She let out a pleased sound upon seeing Adaline in Leo's arms. Kit cast a nervous glance at Leo, who was grinning at the woman and shaking his head.

"We call her Hurricane Ivy," Leo said with a smirk. "I called ahead while I was moving the car seat and explained the situation. She can't resist a child for anything in this world. Fair warning, you might be getting a bear hug at any moment."

Ivy. Ethan's mother. Ada's grandmother. She didn't know Ivy well, but in a small town like Owl Creek, it was impossible to be strangers. At the moment, she was barreling toward them like a runaway train.

"Kit! Ethan called over to tell us about your vehicle trouble." Before she could respond, Ivy enveloped Kit in her arms in the tightest of hugs. The smell of lilacs filled her nostrils and she felt a patting sensation on her back.

"Let the girl go, Ivy. She can't breathe," a deep voice barked. Her husband, Jamie, sat in a wheelchair behind Ivy. His expression was jovial.

When Ivy finally let her go, Kit was face-to-face with Ethan's mother, who was smiling at her as if she'd hung the moon. "I'm sorry for smothering you, but I feel like it's been an eternity since I've seen you. And you probably won't remember, but I taught you in Bible class back when you were a wee child. Ethan was in the class too. So was Leo." Ivy dabbed at her eyes with the hem of her coat.

"Of course I remember," Kit said. "You were always so kind to us. And you made learning fun."

Ivy was a sweet and welcoming presence. Kit sensed that her emotion was tied up in the tragic loss of her son. How painful it must be for Ethan's parents to go through the holiday season without their only child. Mother to mother, Kit's heart went out to her.

"And no apology necessary. I needed a hug," Kit admitted. And she truly did. The last few weeks had been draining and extremely challenging. It was an odd feeling not knowing how she would navigate through the rest of her life with limited vision. Every time she tried to tamp down her fear, it rose up again, threatening to choke her. *Lord, please give me a spirit of hope and not fear as I walk into my future. I want to be calm and focused.*

"Why don't we head inside where we can get cozy by the fire?" Jamie suggested, beckoning them with a wave of his hand. He adroitly spun his wheelchair toward the house. For the first time since their arrival, Kit noticed a long ramp situated by the front entrance, providing Jamie with wheelchair access. He quickly maneuvered his way up the ramp and into the house.

When she stepped inside the Duggan home, Kit felt an immediate sense of being surrounded by warmth and coziness. Leo ushered her into the large living room where a crackling fire blazed in the stone fireplace. The room had high timbered ceilings and tall full windows, which gave a bird's eye view of the property. It lent the space a wide-open atmosphere. A gigantic Christmas tree, decorated to the hilt with an assortment of lovely ornaments, sat by a large bay window.

Leo placed Adaline in front of the tree and the little girl gazed up at the Fraser fir with wide eyes. Kit knew her daughter had never seen such a magnificent tree.

"Welcome to our home, Kit," Ivy said, reaching out and squeezing Kit's hand. "Your daughter is adorable. What's her name?" she asked, bending over to caress Ada's cheek.

Kit spoke past a dry throat. "Adaline. I call her Ada for short."

"This handsome man here is my husband, Jamie, in case you didn't know," she said, jerking her chin in the direction of the man behind her. "I'm sure you've seen him here and there."

"Nice to see you again, Kit. Your dad is an old school friend of mine," Jamie said with a smile. "Sorry about your truck, but I'm sure it'll be fixed in no time." With his silver hair and twinkling blue eyes, Jamie exuded a kind air. He also looked a lot like Ethan... and Adaline.

The sound of footsteps on the hardwood floor heralded the arrival of Florence, who walked into the room with two blond-haired toddlers.

"Hey, Kit. It's been a long time." She nodded toward her boys. "These are my sons, Jace and Carl. At the moment they're a little wired up on sugar." She let out a hearty laugh.

"Hi, Florence," Kit said, happy to see her old friend. In their younger days, they'd shared a tight bond that had unraveled over the years. Kit truly missed the days when they would finish each other's sentences. Being close with Jules was wonderful, but she missed having a bunch of friends. "This is my daughter, Adaline," she said. Just saying the words out loud caused a burst of pride to flow through her. She may not have accomplished much in her life, but with God's grace, she had brought this amazing girl into the world.

"She's precious. And she looks a lot like you," Florence said, smiling down at Adaline.

The truth was Adaline didn't resemble Kit at all. But oftentimes people would tell Kit that Ada was her twin. She felt a sense of relief that no clanging bells were going off in Florence's head. Or anyone else's. Perhaps it was Kit's own guilt that caused her to see a massive resemblance between Ada and Ethan.

Adaline was a little bit younger than the twins, but they began to play nicely together with a bunch of items from a toy box. "This is a nice treat for her. She doesn't get a lot of socialization with kids her age," Kit explained.

"They're great boys," Leo said. A tinge of pride laced his voice. "They can be a handful, but they'll be gentle with Ada. And they know how to share." His cell phone buzzed and he walked a few feet away from the group to take the call.

Kit looked around the room. Leo sure hadn't been kidding. A lot of people really did live at the ranch. She still hadn't seen Florence's mother, Renata, and her stepfather, Patrick Duggan. Or Leo's mom, Annie. She imagined that Christmas morning at the Duggan home would be lively.

Family photos were scattered around the living room. Her gaze fixed on a picture of Ethan in his military attire. With dark hair and sky blue eyes, Ethan had been a good-looking man. He'd cut a fine figure in his marine blues. There was a resemblance between the two male cousins, although she'd always thought that Leo was the more attractive of the two.

A quick glance in his direction showed her that Leo still had his ear pressed to his cell phone. As soon as he hung up, he walked over to her. Leo made a face. "I have some good news and some bad news. Which one do you want me to hit you with first?"

Chapter Eight

"**B**ad news first," Kit blurted out. She steeled herself to take on another blow. It couldn't be any worse than the news she'd received from her retinal specialist a few weeks ago, she thought. Something was telling her she had some pricey auto repairs in her future, ones she couldn't afford. Although the vintage shop was successful, both she and Jules had put money into it in order to build up their stock, decorate the shop and establish a nice-sized clientele.

"That was Freddy. He's still doing some diagnostic tests on your truck, so you're not going to be able to head home anytime soon."

Kit gulped. It wasn't horrible news, but she didn't feel right imposing on the Duggans' hospitality any longer. She also didn't feel so confident about driving after the sun went down. "And the good news?"

Leo grinned. "You're invited to stay for dinner and a tour of the property. I'd love to show you some of our horses."

Truthfully, she would love to see all the horses and the rest of the property, but Kit didn't want to feel like an imposition. It was one of the reasons she had been desperate for a service dog. She had no intention of allowing her loved ones to bend over backward seeing to her needs. She had always thrived on being independent and she prayed that she always would.

And having Ada right under her grandparents' noses left her unsettled. It was an eerie feeling, holding on to a secret no one else knew.

"Are you sure?" Kit pressed. "I feel so badly about just dropping in on your family like this."

"There's absolutely nothing to feel bad about," Jamie said as he wheeled over toward her. "I suggest we head out before it gets dark. Then we can have supper when we return." He winked at Kit. "You're in for a treat. Ivy is baking a lasagna."

So that was the delicious aroma floating in the air! Her mouth watered just hearing about it. "How can I say no to lasagna?" she asked, knowing she would look rude by refusing to stay.

"Sounds like a plan," Florence said. "Although I think someone has other ideas." She jerked her chin in the direction of a taupe-colored love seat. Adaline was curled up into a little ball with her thumb tucked solidly in her mouth. She was fast asleep. Kit knew from past experience that nothing short of an earthquake would disturb her slumber.

"Now if that isn't a perfect Christmas cherub," Ivy said, crossing her hands in front of her. She was gazing at Ada as if she were the sun, the moon and the stars. It caused a hitch in her heart just knowing what Ivy didn't. Was there some innate connection Ivy felt for her grandchild?

"She's tuckered out. It's been a long day for her," Kit explained. Adaline had arisen at the crack of dawn and had been going nonstop ever since. It was no small wonder she'd conked out.

"Here," Leo said, handing her a comfy cranberry-colored blanket. "This will make her even cozier."

"I don't have the heart to wake her up," Kit confessed. "As a mother, I've found that some of my worst moments with Adaline occurred when she was awoken from a deep sleep."

"Don't worry. I'll stay with her. I'm great with little ones," Ivy said. "I'll watch over her like a hawk."

Leo was looking at her with an expectant expression. She sensed that he wanted her to trust Ivy to look after Ada. Kit bit on the inside of her cheek. The only people who'd ever watched Ada were solely members of Kit's own family. This would be a first. But, even though she'd spent most of her little girl's life trying to stuff it down, Ivy was kin to Ada. Her very own grandmother. By allowing her to watch her grandchild for a short period of time, Kit would be giving her a gift of sorts. She owed Ivy these precious moments. If circumstances had been different, Ada would be familiar with Ivy and calling her Nana. And Kit wouldn't be consumed with guilt.

"Okay," she agreed with a nod of her head. "That sounds doable. Thank you, Ivy, for suggesting it."

"Oh, it's my pleasure," Ivy gushed, grinning from

ear to ear. "I always dreamed of having a granddaughter of my own."

Ivy's comment gave Kit pause. Was Ivy too overwrought about losing Ethan? Was it cruel of her to dangle Adaline in front of a grieving mother? Or was it evening the scales?

"Let's go, Kit," Leo urged. "Ada will be fine with Aunt Ivy. She couldn't be in better hands." Although Kit believed what Leo was saying, the truth she was hiding from the Duggans made this small matter feel like a huge one. It felt as if she were walking a tightrope while juggling at the same time.

Kit put on her hat and mittens as she followed behind Leo, Jamie, Florence and the twins, heading toward the front door. She had to restrain herself from turning around and scooping Ada up in her protective arms.

With every step she took, Kit prayed that she wasn't making a huge mistake.

Leo was excited to show Kit the vast property he'd grown up on. He didn't have to ask why she was dragging her feet about leaving the house. Kit's connection to Adaline was deep and profound. She was her primary caretaker and protector. Of course, she had a few jitters about leaving her with his aunt Ivy. She was basically a stranger. Thankfully, she'd eased up and agreed to tour the property and leave Adaline back at the house.

He didn't want to examine why the thought of showing Kit a glimpse into his world excited him so much.

There had only been one other time with one other woman when he'd been eager to bring her into his world. He winced. That had all blown up in his face, which was why he was keeping things in the friend zone with Kit. It would hurt too much to lose her friendship if things went south between them.

Kit was eager to take a look at the horses, judging by how quickly she was walking down the road toward the stables. Showing Duggan ranch was one of Leo's all-time favorite activities. This place was in his blood thanks to generations of Duggans who'd come before him and built up the property. Their blood, sweat, tears and sacrifices had given him the privilege of calling this ranch home. In his opinion, everything always looked so picture-perfect at the ranch and this early evening was no exception. A brilliant pale moon hung in the sky, providing illumination as they walked toward the outbuildings. This time of year, it started to get dark at 4:00 p.m. and the sun didn't rise until 10:00 a.m. The limited hours of daylight made the days a little harder. But on a clear night like tonight, the moon shone even brighter.

A big pine wreath graced the door of the stables and twinkling white lights lit up the outdoor enclosure. Renata, Florence's mother, always made sure the ranch was bursting with holiday cheer.

Once they entered the stables, the scent of horses, leather and hay hung in the air. Leo breathed in the familiar aroma. It was as natural to him as the sight of the majestic mountains that greeted him every day. He loved all aspects of ranching—the hard work, the livestock, the sights and smells. His new favorite position was service dog wrangler, he thought with a chuckle. It entailed a lot of work, but he enjoyed it. Leo could live happily being a rancher for the rest of his days.

His mother greeted Kit warmly when they arrived at the stables. She'd been checking in on Tawny's progress like a mother hen. Leo knew she wouldn't cease her efforts until the mare was back to normal. Jace and Carl were racing around the stables with Florence always one step behind them, making sure they weren't up to any of their double-trouble shenanigans.

Horses peeked out of every stall, with the exception of Tawny, who wasn't feeling sociable due to her colic. Leo was hoping to see improvement in her condition over the next few days.

"They're all so beautiful," Kit said in an awestruck tone. She looked over the horses as they walked past each stall.

"This one here is Queenie," Leo said as he opened the stall door, then pulled on the horse's lead and brought her out. "She's a very sweet horse, but she can be standoffish at times." He put his finger to his lips. "Don't tell her I said so, but she can be a little bit of a diva," he whispered.

Kit stepped forward so she was standing closer to the mare. "I don't blame her. She's gorgeous." A sigh slipped past her lips. "I used to love riding," she said as she reached out to stroke Queenie's face. "I miss it. The smells and sounds. I don't think I've ever felt so free as when I was riding a horse. It seemed like I was flying each and every time. That probably sounds silly," she said, ducking her head.

"Not at all," he responded. "I feel the same way. That's why I love it so much." She shot him a grateful smile. It landed smack dab in the center of his chest, sending a jolt straight through him. If a smile from Kit could unnerve him this much, Leo was afraid of what havoc a kiss might wreak.

Well, that's why you're not going to try and kiss her, he thought. He hated thinking poorly of Kit, because she truly appeared to be a good woman, but he wasn't taking any chances. There was a mystery in her past regarding Ada's father, and although he would never dream of gossiping about her, he did wonder about why it was such a tightly held secret. He sensed it was hush-hush for a reason.

As his thoughts wandered, Kit was bonding with Queenie and speaking to her in a low sweet voice.

Queenie likes you," he said, impressed by the way Kit had approached the horse without any hesitancy or fear. "I can tell by the way she's nuzzling your hand. She wants you to touch her."

"Aww, girl, I like you too," Kit said, nuzzling her face against Queenie's mane. "How's Tawny doing? Is she any better?"

"She's been diagnosed with colic and she's showing slight improvement, which is reassuring. Thanks for asking," Leo answered.

Leo sensed from Kit's easy manner with Queenie and her graceful movements that she'd spent a decent amount of time around horses. Her caring nature had been on full display when she'd inquired about Tawny. If she was amenable to it, Leo would love to take her riding on the property one day. It was the best way to see the vast acreage of the Duggan ranch in all its glory.

"If you're up to it, we can go riding one day," Leo suggested. "Queenie is my favorite horse, but I'll let you steal her away from me if you like," he said.

"I'd love that," she said, excitement shimmering in her eyes. In a flash, her expression changed to one of uncertainty. "Sooner rather than later, if that's okay. I worry about my vision getting worse. I'm not sure I'll be able to ride in the future."

Her comment threw him off balance for a moment. The despair in her voice threatened to crack his heart wide open. Leo couldn't imagine all the things that were worrying her about her condition. Her eyes were filled with dread. He moved closer toward her so no one else could overhear him. "Kit, diminished eyesight doesn't mean that you can't ride. Or run. Or soar. We've had many folks over the years come to the ranch with different disabilities…vision loss, wheelchair-bound. Don't ever think you can't still live out your dreams. This medical diagnosis is simply a temporary setback."

Moisture pooled in her eyes and she blinked away the tears. "I keep trying to tell myself that, but it gets scary, especially at night when it's just me and my thoughts. The idea of being shrouded in darkness frightens me." She dabbed at her eyes with her mitten. "I really appreciate you lifting me up. It's encouraging to know that I'll still be able to do things I love."

"Of course you will, Kit. You're only as limited as

your imagination. I'm not trying to minimize what you're going through, but ever since I've known you, you've demonstrated a spirit of resilience. Why would that change now?"

The beginnings of a smile caused her mouth to twitch. "I like your optimistic outlook. It will give me something to hold on to in the coming weeks and months in addition to my faith."

"I'm going to keep reminding you," he said, reaching out and squeezing her hand. Leo should have thought it out before establishing physical contact with Kit. As soon as he touched her, he felt as if their proximity was too close for comfort. A sweet fruity smell drifted toward his nostrils—a light floral perfume that clung to her. Breathing suddenly became a little difficult for him and his chest tightened. Oh, this feeling was familiar. And terrifying.

She was looking up at him with wide eyes and he fought against the desire to fight all her battles for her. *You're not her protector*, he reminded himself. *You're just an old friend. Her service dog trainer. Her teacher.*

He sucked in a deep steadying breath and moved a few steps away from her so he could regain his composure. Leo needed a dose of cold Alaskan air. "Why don't we head over to the barn and check in with Jupiter? It'll give you a chance to meet his mom, Daisy. We can walk the dogs back to the house for the night."

"Is that where they sleep? At the house?" Kit asked, walking out of the stall with him.

"Yes," he said with a nod. "The temperature dips too low for them to comfortably sleep all night out here."

"I'm glad Jupiter has a warm roof over his head at night," she said as Leo opened up the barn doors and both dogs came running. He watched Kit's face light up as Jupiter ran straight to her. She gave him a few directions, which he followed. Jupiter was now treating Kit as his owner, which was a positive step in their relationship. They'd bonded.

They headed back outside with Jupiter and Daisy now part of the group.

"It's getting a little frosty out here," his mother said as she walked beside them, rubbing her mittened hands together. "How are you doing, Kit?"

"I think my bones are frostbitten," Kit admitted with a chuckle. "Alaskan winter nights sure do get cold. Brr." She wrapped her arms around her middle in a self-protective gesture.

"Let's head back," Florence suggested. "It's only going to get colder." She grabbed her sons' hands and clasped them with her own so each one was beside her. Leo was always astounded by how seamlessly his cousin had changed her orderly life to take on the challenges of motherhood. Florence had adopted her boys after the death of their mother, a close friend of hers from her college days.

As they walked back to the house, Kit walked in lockstep beside Leo, inundating him with questions about the innermost workings of the Double D Ranch. It was nice that she was so curious about ranching and their way of life. Ranches weren't commonplace in Alaska, so there was a learning curve for most folks. He couldn't help but notice Florence's curious gaze focused on him and Kit. He sent her a stern look, knowing she was wondering if they were making a romantic connection. The Duggan clan wanted Leo to find his other half and settle down. They'd stopped being subtle about it.

Florence smirked at him and he shook his head at her, trying to discreetly let her know that she was wrong in her thinking about his intentions toward Kit. He didn't want Kit to pick up on any of Florence's looks. His family knew nothing about his disastrous attempt to find love online. He was still too ashamed to explain why he'd been absent from the ranch when his father's medical emergency occurred.

There was no way any of them could understand that he lacked the confidence to step out on a limb of faith and pursue love. None of them had been made such a fool of in the pursuit of a romantic connection. And he'd long ago vowed that he'd never go down that road again.

Chapter Nine

"Your family is wonderful," Kit told Leo as they walked in lock step back toward the house. "They're so supportive and loving."

"They're all right," he said with a playful grin. "I'm really blessed to have them. This Christmas won't be the same without my dad, but I'm trying to make sure it's still special. He was the very epicenter of the Duggan clan. I've always thought it was ironic that his heart gave out on him when he suffered the seizure, yet he had the biggest heart of anyone I've ever known. It might sound trite, but it's true."

"It sounded heartfelt, Leo. With just those few, words you showed me exactly who he was," Kit said, reaching out and tightly grasping his hand. He had to admit it felt nice to hold hands with her, so much so that he didn't want to let go. It wasn't even ruined by the fact that his family was walking behind them, no doubt watching like hawks.

Leo jerked his chin in the direction of the corral as

they walked by its large perimeter. "Most of his best moments were right out there, doing what he loved best. There's something to be said about doing what you love."

"That's what I want to teach Ada," Kit said. "Keep striving. Never stop trying to make your dreams come true."

"She's going to be strong like her mother," Leo said with a smile. "There's no question in my mind."

Being a good mother was Kit's number one goal in life. Leo's affirmation that she was doing something right sent her to the stratosphere. She was grinning so much, Kit felt as if her face might crack wide open.

"It's never been comfortable to talk about my dad, but you're so easy to talk to, Kit."

"I'm glad about that," Kit said. "He sounds like an amazing man. I wish I'd known him better than I did. I only knew him in passing." It didn't surprise her that he'd been a gem of a man. He'd raised his son to be a strong, supportive and caring man of faith.

"He was a larger than life figure to me, but a big teddy bear at the same time." Leo chuckled. "He used to stage these impromptu snowball fights and my mother used to get so mad when he blindsided her. But she couldn't stay angry at him for long. No one could. He was a special type of person everyone adored."

Kit looked over at him and smiled. "It sounds like he left quite a legacy. That's all we can ever hope for. That we make a mark in this world."

Snowflakes began to drift down from the sky, and Kit let out a squeal of excitement. With the Christmas lights from the house twinkling in the distance and the moon glowing so beautifully, it seemed as if she'd stepped into a painting. An Owl Creek Christmas vignette. "It's snowing," she said, opening up her arms and twirling around like a ballerina. Around and around she spun with her arms extended until she felt slightly dizzy.

Leo chuckled at the sight of her. "I've never seen a person get so excited about snow, even little kids."

"Life is about finding pleasure in small moments as well as the bigger ones. That's how I've always lived my life." And she hoped that she would continue to do so, despite her future challenges.

"Amen to that," Leo said as he leaned his head back and caught a snowflake in his mouth. Kit giggled and did the same. Jace and Carl looked up at the sky and opened their mouths wide. They let out cries of excitement as soon as one landed in their mouths. "It's snowing, Mama," one of the boys said. Kit wasn't sure which twin was which. They were equally adorable and precocious.

"Aren't we blessed to see so much of the fluffy white stuff?" Florence asked. The twins nodded enthusiastically before chasing each other toward the house. Florence quickened her pace to catch up to them.

"You know what's fascinating?" Kit asked, turning toward Leo. "Fun fact. No two snowflakes are the same. That's what my mother always says."

"Seems impossible with all the snow we get in Alaska," Leo remarked. "But it's true."

Kit looked behind her to make sure the rest of Leo's

family couldn't overhear her. She still wasn't ready for everyone to know about her medical condition. Kit knew it was only a matter of time until it became obvious, but the very thought of being pitied gnawed at her.

"I've been trying to imprint certain images in my mind's eye, so if the worst happens and I completely lose my sight I'll always have them. Sunsets. Twinkling stars. Snowflakes. I'll be able to hold those memories close to me for all time." Just the thought of doing so made her feel more empowered and less frightened. She was dealing with so many complicated emotions. Fear. Hope. Despair. Being with Leo made her feel happy. His friendship meant the world to her. Talking to him about her innermost feelings felt so natural. If only she could unburden herself to him about Ada's paternity. But she couldn't risk it. It was a heavy truth bomb to lay on him.

"I like hearing you say that, Kit," Leo said. "I think it'll help you get to a place of peace so you can step into the future without fear."

"That's all I want for Christmas," she said. "To have a sense of serenity about what's coming would be such a blessing."

She let out a gasp as they drew closer to the twinkling lights emanating from the Duggans' house. Kit was able to see it much better up close. The lights shimmered and sparkled, providing an incredible display of colors. The house looked majestic and celebratory. There wasn't an inch of the home that wasn't lit up. She wanted to soak it all in. It was dazzling.

"The house looks breathtaking!" Kit gushed. "It's

bursting with Christmas cheer. I'm not sure I've ever seen such a decked out home in all of Owl Creek." The sight of the festive decorations made her want to grin from ear to ear. Ever since she was a little girl, Kit had loved all the trappings of the holidays. The more glittering lights the better as far as she was concerned.

Leo chuckled. "You haven't seen anything yet. The Duggan family loves to celebrate Christmas. Uncle Jamie likes to dress up as Jolly Old Saint Nick for the holiday stroll." He made a face. "When we were kids, he used to ask us to accompany him as his elves." Leo let out a groan. "I'm not sure that I've ever gotten over the embarrassment."

Kit laughed so hard she bent over at the waist and held her side. She slapped her hand over her mouth, but the laughter kept coming. "I remember that. It was actually kind of cute," she said once she'd composed herself. Her lips still twitched with merriment.

When they headed inside the house, Kit quickly sought out Adaline and Ivy. She couldn't wait to be reunited with her daughter. The sight that greeted her when she rushed into the living room was heartwarming. Ivy was sitting on the floor with Ada perched on her lap. The older woman was reading a story to Adaline. Her daughter let out a happy sound as soon as she saw Kit, but she didn't move from her perch.

A short while later, they were all seated at the large mahogany table in the dining room eating the most delectable lasagna she'd ever tasted. Florence's parents, Renata and Patrick, had joined them, adding to the convivial vibe. By the time dinner was over, Freddy had driven her fixed truck over to the Duggans' house.

"Thanks so much for the hospitality you've shown me and Adaline," Kit said to the Duggans as she prepared to head home before it got too dark. Thankfully, she would be able to make it home with enough light to safely guide her.

"Come back soon, Kit. Any friend of Leo's is always welcome here," Annie said, reaching out and giving her a hug.

"And bring this little lady back to us," Ivy said, placing a kiss on Adaline's temple. "We'd love to see both of you." Ada smiled up at Ivy. It was a little startling to Kit since it always took her daughter a long time to warm up to people. She must've bonded with Ivy during their time alone.

"I hope to see you at the holiday stroll," Kit said. And she meant it. Even though she still had anxiety about the secret she was keeping, she'd fully enjoyed spending time with the Duggans. They were a lovely family.

"I'll see you out," Leo said, walking Kit and Adaline to the front door amid a chorus of goodbyes from his family.

"Thanks for everything," Kit said as she turned toward him to say goodbye. She looked down at Ada. "Say goodbye to Leo, sweetie."

Adaline lifted her palm to her lips, then blew a kiss to Leo. He put his hand out and made a big show of catching Ada's kiss, then putting it in his pocket. The gesture endeared him to Kit. Anyone who took such pains to interact with her daughter was special.

On the ride home, Kit wrestled over her moral dilemma. As a woman of faith, she knew it wasn't right to hide Ada's paternity from Ethan's loved ones. The Duggans were a wonderful family. They'd all welcomed her into their home with open arms and shown her true hospitality. She knew in her gut that if they knew Ethan was Ada's father, her little girl would be treated with love and warmth. But there would also be anger directed at her, along with a host of questions as to why she had withheld the truth. Kit wasn't sure she would have answers for them. All her actions had been based on fear and shame. After Ethan died, Kit had often wondered if God had been punishing her for being so weak about telling him he'd fathered Adaline.

Now that she knew without question that the Duggans were good people, could she truly justify keeping Ada from them? Her little girl was a direct tie to their beloved Ethan. Fear threatened to consume her. This situation had always been so overwhelming for her. Sometimes Kit had the sensation of her body being swallowed up by quicksand.

How would she ever find a way to come clean to Ethan's family as well as her own?

Leo spent the next few days away from Owl Creek checking out possible new horses for the ranch at an auction. Uncle Patrick had come along with him, and together they'd made the decision to purchase two midnight-colored stallions and one chestnut mare. Spending time with his uncle served as a balm for all the emotions stirred up by the anniversary of his father's death. Uncle Patrick and his father had always been close, so in a sense, Leo felt more connected to both of them.

The entire time he tried not to think about how he'd first met Dahlia at a similar horse auction in Fairbanks where she'd accompanied her father. They'd continued to develop their relationship online in the months following their in person meeting. Despite those painful memories, he focused on the business of acquiring horses for the ranch. He was tired of wallowing over past hurts.

Although it had been a great trip, Leo was eager to get back to Owl Creek. The holiday stroll was only days away, and he'd committed to participating with his service dogs and their owners. All of his past trainees he'd reached out to had been enthusiastic. Now, he needed to talk to Kit after their session and make sure she was able to join in. He was looking forward to it, especially since it would be the first time in ages that he'd been in a social setting. Owl Creek was full of down-to-earth, caring folks who'd created a wonderful community. For the last year, he'd been steeped in grief. Leo had made a vow to be more involved in the goings-on in his hometown. There was no better time to engage than right now during the holiday season.

When Kit showed up at the ranch for their session, Leo realized he'd missed working with her while he'd been out of town. He'd gotten used to seeing her regularly and deepening their friendship. Kit's sweet personality appealed to him. She was a burst of sunshine on the rainiest of days. And in the last year and a half there had been a lot of rainy days he'd endured.

Leo had to hand it to Jupiter. He was teaching him a lot about making premature judgments. The plucky Labrador retriever was out performing all the other dogs he'd trained in the program. He was learning each task at a much faster rate than his siblings and working in sync with Kit's needs. Jupiter had sure shown him that he didn't know half as much as he thought he did. It was fitting that Kit was paired up with a high-achieving pup. God was looking out for her, whether she realized it or not.

"Jupiter is breezing through the training, so I think it's time we step things up since his main job will be to help you out with tasks and to make sure you avoid dangerous situations. I know you've had some falls recently, so that's important work. Public access training will be really important as you go to work, do grocery shopping, among other things," Leo explained.

"I'm really looking forward to it. Jupiter is so smart, Leo," Kit said, beaming. "I think he can handle anything we throw at him."

Leo loved how proud Kit was of Jupiter. It spoke well of their budding relationship. They made a terrific team and their bond would only grow stronger with time. They would lean on each other. Grow with one another.

"By the way, Beulah has asked for participation from my service dogs and their owners for the holiday stroll. It's a nice way to showcase the program and spread awareness." He grinned at Kit. "I may be biased, but this group of dogs are pretty good-looking."

"I can only speak to Jupiter's good looks. Honestly, if being a service dog doesn't work out, he could definitely be a cover model for doggy magazines," Kit said, grinning.

"So, I know Jupiter isn't officially your dog as of yet, but I wanted you to walk with the group and lead Jupiter. As you know, it's a fun town event, so this will make it even more memorable. I know it's short notice, but it's pretty straightforward."

Kit retreated within herself right before his eyes. She broke eye contact with him and fidgeted with her parka's zipper instead of looking at him. "I—I'm sorry, Leo. I'm not really interested in doing that."

Leo let Kit's comment marinate for a moment. He hadn't expected this response from her. Was this about a work conflict?

"Can you tell me why? We can work around whatever you're doing with the shop."

She shook her head. Her features were pinched. "It's not that."

He met her gaze and waited for her to explain what was going on. Perhaps it was him she was trying to avoid.

"I don't want everyone to know," she said in a low voice. "Okay?" she asked in a curt tone.

"That you need a service dog?" he prodded. He must have misunderstood. Kit had begged him to be in his service dog program. It made no sense that she was ashamed to be associated with it. For Leo, it would feel like an insult to all the hours and hard work he'd put into his program. Not to mention a slight to Jupiter.

"That I'm losing my sight. And yes, that I'll be dependent on Jupiter." Her mouth settled into a firm thin line. "It's not something I want to announce with a neon sign even though it's getting more and more obvious."

He counted to ten in his head. "Kit, it may not be my business, but it feels like you're running away from your reality. Sooner or later everyone in Owl Creek is going to know about your condition. You're doing something brave. Why try to hide it?"

"I'm not brave, Leo. I'm actually a coward," she muttered.

"That's not true," he said with a frown. "Why would you say that?" Kit was heroic in his eyes. As a single mother. As someone facing a terrifying diagnosis. As a business owner living out her dreams. Frankly, he wished that he'd faced the world head-on when his father and Ethan passed away. Instead, he had hidden himself away at Duggan ranch, retreating into his own world.

"What do you think I'm known for in Owl Creek?" She spit out the question with a hint of anger flashing in her eyes.

Being kind and beautiful with sparkling green eyes the color of emeralds, he wanted to say. Nope, he wasn't heading into any minefields. Not today.

"For being a wonderful person," he said, managing to speak despite the lump in his throat.

"No, that's incorrect. When people hear the name

Kit O'Malley, they think of a single mother raising a baby without a father."

Leo let out a shocked sound. "Kit! Give people more credit. Sure, a few people might think of you in that way, but so many more hold you in high esteem. That's why you should keep your head up high and stroll with us."

Kit snatched her bag from where she'd placed it. "Leo, I don't want to be pushed into anything. Everything in my life is out of control right now and I don't need to be pressured."

"I'm only trying to encourage you to see things from a different perspective. I'm sorry if that came across as pushy."

"I'm doing the best I can to keep my head above water. It's exhausting," she said, her voice trembling. Up to this point, she'd appeared as if she was handling everything exceedingly well. But, clearly she wasn't.

"You've been through a lot. Please know that I'm well aware of that. And I completely empathize with you," he said in a soft voice.

Her eyes widened. "I don't want your pity, Leo. That's the last thing I require or need. From you or anyone else in this town." Kit grabbed her belongings and turned away from him. A sneaking suspicion told him she was done with their conversation.

"Kit! Wait. Don't leave!" he called out when he realized she intended to take off.

In the space of a few seconds, Kit stormed out of the barn without turning back toward him.

By the time Leo thought to go after her, Kit had already sped away. He felt stunned by the sudden shift in their conversation and what had been revealed to him.

Leo stared after her truck and ran a hand across his jaw. *What had just happened?* He couldn't help but feel a little wounded. Leo hadn't been making her into an object of pity in the slightest. Ever since the first time she'd walked into his barn, he'd tried to be a sounding board and a good friend. Clearly, that didn't mean anything to her. It hurt way more than he wanted to acknowledge.

He wasn't sure he really knew Kit after all.

Ten minutes later on her ride back to town, Kit burst into tears. She had been feeling so positive and hopeful lately. Now, in the span of a few minutes, she'd lost her cool. And she'd made a fool of herself in the process. All her fears and insecurities had been triggered at the idea of everyone in Owl Creek learning about her situation. It didn't make any sense even to her. All she knew was that for once she wanted her name to be associated with an achievement like opening Second Time Around with Jules. It was ridiculous to feel this way since being in the dog service program with Jupiter had been an answer to a prayer. It had given her hope. Leo's friendship had been such a gift. The road blurred before her eyes as emotion took over. Kit pulled her truck over to the side of the road so she could collect herself.

Had she lost Leo as a friend with her outburst? Kit dabbed at her eyes and let out a groan filled with regret. If only she could go back in time and take back her actions. Why hadn't she simply told him in a calm and collected manner that she didn't feel comfortable participating? All her anger and frustration she had been bottling up over the past few weeks had come out in her conversation with Leo.

By the time Kit arrived at the shop, she had managed to calm herself down and dry her tears. As she entered the store and locked gazes with Jules, her sister immediately saw straight through her. At the moment, Second Time Around was in a lull with no customers. For the first time ever, Kit was thankful for no shoppers.

"What's wrong? You look upset," Jules said, walking toward her and scrutinizing her face. "You've been crying. Your eyes are red."

"It's nothing," Kit said. "I just butted heads with Leo after our session."

Jules raised her eyebrows. "Really? He's like the nicest guy on the planet. What were you arguing about?"

Kit shrugged. "He asked me to participate in the holiday stroll with a group of service dogs and their owners as well as himself. And he kept probing when I turned down the invite." Just saying it out loud made her feel ridiculous. She'd gotten upset over such a small issue.

Jules frowned. "That doesn't sound like something to get worked up about."

Kit sank down onto a comfy taupe-colored love seat. She'd hand-selected the beautiful piece for the store, knowing it would add to the vintage chic decor. "I don't know what set me off so much."

"Don't you?" Jules asked, sitting down next to her. "From what I've noticed, you care a lot about what people think. It started with your pregnancy. You shrank down inside yourself out of shame. It took you a while to see that Adaline was a gift from God."

She nodded solemnly. "Once she was born, I knew she would always be the center of my world. It's hard to see blessings when you're in pain," she admitted. Being pregnant as a single woman had been a frightening and isolating experience. She winced as memories of disclosing her pregnancy to her parents crashed over her. It had been one of the most humbling experiences of Kit's life.

"I blew up on Leo because of my pride," she admitted. "And I regret it. Leo has my back. He's been a good friend and ally in my darkest hour."

Jules shot her a pointed look. "Just a friend?"

Kit bristled. "Of course. Why would you ask that?"

"I don't know, Kit. To be honest, something feels off. You and I are as close as can be, yet you've never told me the identity of Adaline's father." She knit her brows together. "And you resisted at first going to see Leo at the ranch when I first told you about the service dog lessons." She narrowed her gaze. "Honestly, I can't help but wonder…is Leo Adaline's father?"

Chapter Ten

Kit let out a startled gasp. Jules's question had come out of the blue, shocking Kit to her core. She sputtered. "Leo! You think Leo is my child's father?"

"I don't know what to think. Leo is the only person who makes sense. You've been spending a lot of time at the ranch working with him. I sense that the two of you share a special bond." Jules lifted her hands in the air. "What else am I to think?"

A special bond? Yes, Kit couldn't deny it. Their friendship was genuine and one of a kind. She'd never known anything like it.

"Leo is an amazing man," Kit acknowledged. "But he is not Adaline's father. If he were, Leo would have claimed her as his daughter. That's the sort of man he is."

"You're right. But if he isn't, then who is? It's time you told me, Kit." Jules's eyes pleaded with her for the truth.

It was time. Her own shame had kept her silent for

such a long time. Jules had always been a loving and loyal sister. If she couldn't trust Jules, then whom could she believe in?

Kit lifted her chin up and met her sister's gaze head-on. "Adaline's father is a Duggan, Jules. Just not Leo. Her father is Ethan."

If her sister hadn't been sitting down, Kit suspected she might be picking her up off the floor right about now. Seconds ticked by without Jules uttering a single word.

"A-are you all right?" Kit asked. "You look a bit rattled."

"I just need a moment to process this." She scratched her jaw. "Ethan? When? How? I mean not how, but I had no idea the two of you were even in each other's orbit."

"We really weren't. He came home for a leave. I think he was back for a few weeks and we ended up hanging out after volunteering at the youth center. It sounds trite but one thing led to another. He went back overseas and a few months later I realized I was pregnant." She let out a brittle laugh. "When I finally summoned the courage to tell him, I discovered he was engaged to someone he'd recently met. A fellow soldier. Rebecca."

"So you didn't tell him you were pregnant?" Jules asked, sounding a bit stunned.

"No, I didn't. I honestly had no way to contact him once he left town. And when Ada was born, I decided to reach out to him. I knew he had a right to know he was a father and to love her as his very own." Kit's lip

quivered. "But then he was killed overseas and it hit me
that I'd waited too long." She let out a sob. "I'll never
get the opportunity to let him hold his baby girl. Even
though he was overseas, I know Ethan would have done
just about anything to meet her. Adaline might never
forgive me. Why did I wait?"

Jules reached out and wrapped her arms around Kit.
She rubbed her back and whispered, "You had no way
of knowing he was going to pass away. What happened to Ethan was a tragedy that no one could have
predicted."

Kit nodded. What Jules said was true. Never in a
million years had she imagined that Ethan would lose
his life so tragically. At the time, it had brought Kit
to her knees.

"I feel so guilty when I'm with Leo at the ranch," Kit
confessed. "He doesn't deserve to have the truth withheld from him." She paused to take a breath. "The Duggans have been so kind to me. They met Ada the day
my truck broke down. Ethan's mom treated her like one
of her own."

"She is," Jules said. "She's her granddaughter. Maybe
on some level she senses a connection to Ethan."

"I need to tell her. Actually, it's important that they
all know." Truth was the only way to navigate her way
through this situation. Deep down she'd always known
that a moment of reckoning would be upon her. "It's
only right. Ada is a living link to Ethan."

"Oh, Kit. I know it's going to be hard, but I'll be
right by your side if you like. You won't have to do it
alone." Jules leaned in and smoothed back her hair.

"Jules, I might take you up on that," Kit said. "I have a lot to answer for. I don't imagine Ethan's family will be very happy with me."

"Don't focus on that at the moment," Jules said, tightly squeezing her hand. "Keep your eyes on the goal of full disclosure."

For some reason, Leo's face popped into her mind. She cared so very much about his good opinion of her. And it gutted her to imagine that their friendship would be destroyed by her bombshell news about his cousin.

Leo awoke to a sky devoid of sunshine. Sunrise wouldn't be occurring for a few hours. During this time of the year, sunlight was limited. Leo grinned as he looked outside his bedroom window at the blanket of snow covering the ground. Having a fresh layer of snow would make the holiday stroll even more festive. Visions of peppermint mocha hot chocolate served up by the Snowy Owl Diner began to dance in his head. His empty stomach began to grumble at the thought of all the delicious goodies he would consume at the festive event.

Giving himself extra time to sleep in had been a good decision. He needed to get some more rest instead of working himself to the bone. He'd thrown himself into extra work around the ranch in order to take his mind off the anniversary of his father's death. In the process, he'd burnt himself out. Attending Owl Creek's most festive event of the year would be even more special due to the abundance of snow that had fallen.

He'd been trying not to think about Kit since their

tension-filled incident from the other day. She'd canceled her last session under the guise of not feeling well so he hadn't seen her in a few days. Could she really be that upset with him? The thought of losing their friendship wrecked him. Leo didn't know what to think. Maybe he should have called her or gone to Second Time Around to check in on her. Leo hadn't reached out to her at all. He was still a little taken aback at how strained things had gotten between them.

After digging into a hearty breakfast, Leo headed down to the stables to check in on Tawny before heading to the holiday event. As soon as he saw the horse, Leo knew she had turned a corner in her recovery.

"Hey, girl. You look so much better than the other day," he crooned, smoothing back the mare's mane. Leo chuckled as Tawny whinnied and nudged him with her nose. "You just made my day. Do you know that?" Leo grinned all the way back to the house. Tawny's recovery was something to rejoice about.

As soon as his mother was ready to go, Leo put Jupiter and Daisy in the back of his truck so they could head into town. Daisy wasn't a service dog, but he reckoned she deserved an outing due to the fact that she'd birthed all the pups. Snow-covered Sitka trees greeted them on the way along with the prettiest view of white-topped mountains.

"I'm so excited to help out with the pies this year," his mother said. "It'll be a nice distraction." She didn't need to elaborate. They were all trying to push through the holiday season and find joy.

"Save me a slice of pecan or blackberry if you can," he said. "Piper's pies are usually sell outs."

"Pie in the Sky, is one of the best things to happen in Owl Creek, along with the chocolate company, Ace's dog rescue and now your service dog program." She reached over and squeezed his arm. "Your father would be so proud of all the folks you're helping. That was a big part of his life. Reaching out to those in need."

Leo nodded. "It's unexpected, but lately I can think of him without feeling as if my insides are being torn apart. I'm actually starting to smile when I remember certain moments. We had so many good times. Our family was truly blessed."

"That's called healing, son. Day by day, we get a little bit stronger. And what I've come to realize is that nothing can take away our memories. And you're right. We were so fortunate to have your dad and Ethan in our lives."

"Amen," Leo said. They settled into a companionable silence as the picturesque Alaskan landscape provided the perfect panorama. His mother let out a contented sigh. Main Street was bursting with all the trimmings of an Owl Creek Christmas. A tall majestic Christmas tree sat proudly in the middle of the town green. Vendors were already setting up their tables, and children were taking advantage of small hills to sled down. The vibe was one of joy and expectation. Leo couldn't wait to be a part of the celebration. He let his mother out in front of the Snowy Owl Diner with Daisy, then headed off to find a place to park.

Leo found his gaze landing on Second Time Around

as he drove past the vintage store. The windows were beautifully decorated in keeping with the holiday season. Kit and Jules had gone all out to make their establishment merry and bright. Wreaths were hung on all the shop doors along with signs celebrating the holiday stroll. Today's event was a boon for all the local businesses, as well as an opportunity for the Owl Creek community to support their endeavors. He slowed his truck down when he spotted Kit walking out of the shop dressed in a red peacoat and a matching knit hat. Leo quickly navigated his truck to an available parking spot, then pulled down the back hatch so the dog could jump down.

"Kit!" he called out, hoping to catch up to her so they could clear the air. He didn't like being at odds with people, especially someone as special as Kit.

She turned at the sound of her name, looking straight at him before ducking her head and scooting around the corner.

"Oh, come on. This is beyond ridiculous," he said out loud. He looked down at Jupiter. "Am I right, Jupe?" Jupiter cocked his head to the side. "Good thing I know this area like the back of my hand." As kids, he and Ethan had discovered every shortcut imaginable in the area as they played superheroes. Ethan had always loved those moments. Cherished memories were surrounding him like a cozy blanket, serving as a reminder that love endured loss.

Leo cut her off at the pass by walking at a fast clip through a Christmas tree lot and beating her to the corner of Main and Elm. Kit stopped short as soon as she saw him and Jupiter directly in front of her. He quickly closed the distance between them. He was standing so close to her so there was no way she could avoid looking him straight in the eye.

"Kit. Fancy meeting you here. I hope you're not avoiding me. Or Jupiter," he said, nodding his chin toward the pup.

"I'm not," Kit said, shaking her head. "Why would I?"

Leo raised an eyebrow. "Really? It pretty much feels like it. We haven't seen you in days."

"Well, perhaps I have been, just a little," she admitted. A sheepish expression was stamped on her face.

"I knew it," he said. "Jupiter misses training with you."

Kit reached down and began stroking the dog. "The feeling is mutual."

"No matter what went down between us, you have to continue your training with Jupiter," Leo urged. "You're going to need him, Kit. You made a commitment when you signed up, and you have to honor that." End of lecture. He needed Kit to understand that the only way she would get to the finish line with Jupiter was by doing the necessary work.

She nodded. "I understand. For what it's worth, I've been feeling really foolish about our argument. I was upset about other things, and it all landed on you. That wasn't right or fair." She let out a groan and covered her face with her mittened hands. "I was so ashamed of my outburst that I couldn't face you. You've been nothing but wonderful to me."

"You're a good person, Kit O'Malley. I certainly

wouldn't hold one difficult moment against you. Now that wouldn't be fair, would it?"

Kit let out a sigh. "Leo, you're the fairest person I've ever known. Bar none. Which is why I've reconsidered my position." Kit crossed her hands in front of her. "I want to walk with your group this afternoon. Matter of fact, there's nothing I'd like more."

"What? Are you serious?" he asked, surprised by the sudden turn of events. "I wasn't expecting you to change your mind."

She bobbed her head. "Honestly, neither was I. But just seeing you and Jupiter reminded me that I need to be brave. I can't let myself worry so much about how people regard me." Her voice trembled. "And I refuse to be ashamed of my journey. Your service dog training is a huge part of it. I want to acknowledge that today."

"Are you sure?" he asked, feeling incredulous at her change of heart. "There's no pressure to participate, although we'd love for you to join us. It's all about showcasing the program in a positive light and having fun."

"I'm absolutely sure," Kit said. "I just need to pick up a coffee for Jules and then head back and tell her my plans for the afternoon."

"What about the shop? I know a lot of sales happen today."

"We've been doing a brisk business this morning, so our plan was to close early so we can enjoy the festivities."

"Sounds good. Let me walk you over to the coffee shop, then we can meet up later on with the group," Leo said as euphoria washed over him. He didn't want to dwell on why he suddenly had a sense as if all was right in his world. As they walked side by side down the street with Jupiter leading the way, Leo felt happier than he had in a very long time.

With a sinking sensation in his gut, Leo knew it had everything to do with Kit. She was changing his world with her plucky outlook and tender heart. Her friendship made him want to venture out more and to make the most of his life. It was an exhilarating yet terrifying feeling. Leo was starting to need her in a way that reminded him of his promise not to get caught up again in his feelings for a woman. Red warning lights were flashing all around him. He needed to proceed with caution.

Kit quickly walked back to Second Time Around after parting ways with Leo at the Coffee Bean. As soon as she entered the shop, Kit explained to her sister that she'd had a change of heart about walking with the service dog folks.

"I'm so happy you're strolling with Leo's group," Jules said, beaming as she sipped from her peppermint mocha coffee Kit had just purchased. Little vapors of heat were rising from the top and a minty aroma hung in the air. "It'll be good for you to put yourself out there."

"Are you sure you'll be okay until closing?" Kit asked. Lately, Jules had accommodated her service dog training hours. She didn't want to take advantage of her sister's kindness.

"Of course I will," Jules said, shooing her away with

her hand. "I hate to ask, but will you be all right? I know you said your field of vision has shifted a little bit."

"It has. Driving has gotten more challenging, as well as seeing things in sharp focus at a distance," she answered with a sigh. "I have an eye appointment scheduled for a few days after Christmas. I've decided to go ahead with treatment. It's minimally invasive and the rewards outweigh any potential risks."

"Oh, Kit. That's amazing. I'll do anything you need to support you. In the meantime, enjoy yourself and don't worry." She shook her finger at Kit. "I know how your mind works."

"I promise to live in the moment and not stress out," Kit vowed. And she would try her best as difficult as it might be. "I'll look for you in the crowd. I can't wait to show off Jupiter."

"I'll be there," Jules said, holding her cup up in the air in acknowledgment. "Clapping extra loud."

With a wave and a grin, Kit walked out of the shop and headed to the assigned meeting place that Leo had mentioned—the parking lot for the Snowy Owl.

As Kit headed down Main Street, she was able to get a glimpse of the town's festive decorations. Kit stopped on several occasions to gaze at shop windows. Each looked more festive than the next. Red ribbons and candy canes. Glitzy tinsel and shimmering gold stars. The toy shop had a gorgeous red sled with silver ribbons tied to the sides. Kit smiled at the thought of the happiness it might bring on Christmas morning. Adaline was too small for such a gift, but she was looking forward to one day seeing her daughter fly down a hill with the wind flowing through her hair. Kit hoped she would retain enough of her vision so this moment would be possible. There were no guarantees.

By the time Kit arrived at the lot, a small group had assembled with Leo at the center. He had both Daisy and Jupiter with him. Every time she saw him, Kit felt a little bit breathless. With every passing second, Kit was feeling guiltier about withholding the truth from Leo and his family. She was almost at a breaking point, knowing she was close to blurting out her secret.

As soon as he saw her, Leo beckoned her over to join the group. In a small town like Owl Creek, no introductions were needed. She knew all the members—Trudy Miller, Otis Cummings, Ronnie Lake and Regina Lawson. Everyone greeted her enthusiastically and introduced their service dogs to her. Kit got a kick out of meeting Jupiter's four siblings. They were all adorable and lively pups. Kit couldn't help but feel she'd gotten the pick of the litter with Jupiter.

"You remember Daisy, or as I like to call her, Mama Bear." Leo beamed at the sweet Labrador who was a true warrior. Kit knew all about Daisy being abandoned by her owner in the woods and nearly losing her life before delivering her litter. It was a powerful story that highlighted Daisy's strength and the wonderful care provided by Maya Reynolds and her veterinarian clinic.

"Of course I do. I could never forget such a beautiful dog," Kit said, admiring the dog's glistening coat and calm demeanor. "She's a sweetheart."

"She's a special one," Leo said, smiling as he lovingly patted her. Something is his tone betrayed his deep affection for the dog. She imagined that after all the loss he'd endured, Daisy had been a blessing. A light in the darkness.

A syrupy smell reminiscent of caramel apples wafted in the air, reminding Kit of all the goodies that were being sold by dozens of vendors. Her favorite treat were the cinnamon sugar donuts from the Snowy Owl. She made a mental note to bring half a dozen home to her family.

Kit let out a groan. "These aromas are incredibly tempting."

Leo began to sniff the air around them. "I smell fried dough and French fries. Two of my all-time favorites."

"Oh, you're making me even hungrier," she said, rubbing her belly and making a tortured face.

"Sorry about that," he said, chuckling. "How about I promise to feed you later? We can grab some food from one of the vendors or eat at the diner."

"I'm going to hold you to it," Kit said, excited at the prospect of hanging out with Leo away from the ranch.

Something was brewing between them that felt deeper than friendship, but she couldn't allow herself to fully explore it. She ought to thank the Lord above for bringing someone like Leo into her world at one of the most trying times of her life. He was a steady force who she could lean on. Anything else would be disastrous.

"It's show time," Trudy called out, her excitement evident in her tone.

Kit surveyed the group of service dogs. Much like a proud papa, Leo had bragged about their accomplishments. Trudy's dog, Artemis, had been trained to detect low blood sugar levels. Frisco, a hearing dog, alerted his owner to noises such as alarms, horns and doorbells. Sheba was a mobility assistance dog, performing tasks for her wheelchair-bound owner. Woody was a seizure support dog, alerting his owner to imminent seizures.

The group formed two lines and joined the procession walking down Main Street. Ace and Maya were walking in front of them with a few of their rescue dogs who were up for adoption. The mood was celebratory and festive.

Kit waved to her family in the crowd as she led Jupiter around the town green. Pride bubbled up inside her when Adaline pointed at her and called out "Mama." Her daughter wouldn't remember this moment, but Kit liked to think she was showing her a bit of resilience. Despite her setbacks, Kit was determined to forge ahead and stay positive.

She couldn't stop smiling at the warm reception their group was receiving from the crowd. Tad was jumping up and down, yelling out Jupiter's name. Leo walked beside her with Daisy, giving high fives to several kids as they walked past.

Beulah North, the grand dame of Owl Creek, was dressed up in a red and white Mrs. Claus outfit and handing out bars of chocolate from her company, North Star Chocolate Shop. Her husband, Jennings, stood beside her dressed up as Santa Claus. Beulah gave them a thumbs-up as they walked by her. Getting a stamp of approval from the town's matriarch meant a lot to Kit.

For the most part, Jupiter listened to her commands and was on his best behavior. He still needed to be introduced to public access training, so Kit was pleased with how he'd acted in a crowded setting.

As soon as the procession ended, Tad flew to her side and wrapped his arms tightly around her. Seconds later, her parents walked over with Ada in their arms. Her daughter wriggled and held up her arms so Kit could scoop her up. She managed to hold Jupiter's leash while propping her daughter on her hip. A few minutes later, Ada was rubbing her eyes and fussing.

"Why don't we take her home for a nap?" her dad suggested. "She's been fighting the sandman for the last hour so she could see you and Jupiter."

Kit pressed a kiss on Ada's forehead. "Oh, no, Dad. I want you to enjoy the day. Maybe I should just head home with her," Kit said. As it was, she always felt as if she was balancing her work and training hours against spending quality time with Ada. Being a working mother was a juggling act.

"Don't you dare!" her mother chided. "Your father and I will head home and you can stay on. You deserve some downtime."

Kit reached out and hugged her mother. "Thank you. I've been having a great time." And she was! All the sights and the sounds of the town's holiday event were being stored away in her mind. The colors and the glistening tinsel. The magnificent lights. She wasn't going to let herself think about the fact that this might be her last Christmas seeing all of these sights in vivid color. She was determined to live in the moment.

By the time she said her goodbyes, Adaline was fast asleep on her grandpa's shoulder.

Kit couldn't count the number of people on one hand who approached her after the parade and asked her about working with Jupiter. After the first few inquiries, Kit felt more comfortable and relaxed about being open and honest about Jupiter being trained as her guide dog. Nobody seemed to be judging her. The townsfolk were supportive and understanding about her condition. Many revealed their own medical situations and wondered if they too could benefit from a service animal.

A little while later, Leo found her in the throng of people. "Thanks for being a part of this, Kit. Honestly, I don't think it could have gone any better judging by the reaction from the townsfolk."

She looked up at Leo, warmed by his gratitude. In reality, she should be thanking him for his patience and grace. Walking with Jupiter had been wonderful and empowering. "Thanks for asking me, even though Jupiter and I haven't graduated yet."

"You're well on your way. You might end up being my most successful team." He quirked his mouth. "If you don't bail on any more sessions, that is. Consistency is very important for a service animal."

"I appreciate you looking past my behavior the other day." She locked gazes with Leo, wanting him to see the sincerity in her eyes. She wasn't going to blow this golden opportunity to go the distance with Jupiter. She should have just shown up for training and apologized. "I won't miss any more classes. That's a promise, Leo. Even when I'm feeling a little down in the dumps about what's coming, it helps me to know that Jupiter will be assisting me. I can't overstate that enough."

Leo had been understanding about her outburst, which seemed to be a hallmark of his personality. For some reason it made her feel a bit unworthy of his time and attention. He was such a sincere person, one who was levelheaded and open at all times. His transparency put her to shame. It made her wish she'd done the right thing in the past and been honest with the Duggans.

Was it ever too late to tell the truth? At this point, it was the only way to achieve redemption.

"So, why don't we check out the food tents?" Leo suggested, interrupting her thoughts. "I haven't eaten since breakfast, so I'm starving."

"I'm more than ready," Kit said. Her stomach had been rumbling so loudly it was a little embarrassing.

"Wait a second. Where are the dogs?" Kit asked, looking around for the two Labrador retrievers.

"My mom took them back to the ranch," Leo explained. "Jupiter did a fantastic job, but I don't want to overstimulate him with so many people milling about."

"Jupiter's a rock star," Kit said. "And so is his mom."

"You won't get any argument from me," Leo said. "Well, let's go while the goings good. Temps are supposed to drop this evening so I heard things might be wrapping up earlier than expected."

"If you want, we can also do a little Christmas shopping. I'm so behind on gifts."

"Good idea," Leo said, grinning. "Maybe we can go halfsies on a gift for Jupiter. Ace told me the dog rescue was setting up a tent and selling dog treats and toys."

"I'd love that," Kit said, feeling way more excited than she should about spending time with Leo.

This isn't a date, she reminded herself. *Stop getting all fluttery and weak in the knees*. She and Leo were in the friendship zone. He was her buddy, not a prospective boyfriend. Then why was her pulse racing so fast? Why did it seem as if she was as nervous as she'd always been on the first day of school?

Why did it feel as if she might be heading into dangerous waters simply by being around Leo?

Chapter Eleven

Christmas was on full display as Leo and Kit walked around the square. No detail had been overlooked by the holiday stroll committee. Garlands, wreaths and red bows hung from every lamppost and building. A majestic tree sat in the middle of the town green. In Leo's opinion, it was even more magnificent than last year. It was an Owl Creek tradition to turn the lights on at the conclusion of the evening as the entire town looked on in delight. Ever since he was a little tyke, Leo had considered it the climactic part of the event.

Every few steps they would stop to talk to one of the townsfolk or a friend wishing them a Merry Christmas. For Leo, it was nice to be out and about again. When they crossed paths with Beulah, she greeted them with warm hugs and complimented them on their contribution to the event.

"Leo, I'd like to talk to you about your service dog training after the holidays," Beulah said with a grin.

"I would love to give you some funding for future endeavors."

"That would be incredible," Leo said, surprised by Beulah's comment. For a while now he'd been thinking about expanding the program. "I'll definitely reach out to you after Christmas."

"You do that, young man," Beulah said with a wink. "Carry on and enjoy yourselves. The holiday stroll only comes around once a year."

As Beulah walked away, Leo looked over at Kit. "Did I just imagine that Beulah wants to finance my little service dog training venture?"

"I heard the same thing as you," Kit said, patting him on the shoulder. "It's so exciting. Congratulations, Leo."

"I won't celebrate yet, but it sounds promising," Leo said. Being touched by Kit even in the most platonic of ways still caused a little hitch in his heart. Was it only him feeling the chemistry? Not that he was in any frame of mind to pursue her romantically, but he did wonder if she harbored even the slightest attraction to him.

It was amazing how everything in his life was beginning to look brighter. He still grieved for Ethan and his father, but he felt happier than he had in ages. A few minutes later, they came across a bakery table overflowing with treats from the Snowy Owl Diner. Just watching Kit's face light up with pleasure as she spotted her favorite cinnamon-flavored donuts was enjoyable. He had no idea why her joy made him feel as if all was right in his world.

After they split a donut and Kit ate one more by herself, she purchased a half dozen to take home. "Are you sure those donuts are going to make it back to your family?" he teased.

Kit threw back her head in laughter. "I'm not even going to pretend to be insulted. There's a good chance of my nibbling on another one before they reach their final destination."

Leo chuckled along with her. She looked even more beautiful when she was happy. What would it be like, he imagined, to be the man who made Kit smile for the rest of her days? Leo wasn't sure if he was being paranoid, but it seemed as if they were getting their fair share of curious stares and a few whispers to boot. He prayed Kit didn't notice. She'd already told him about her insecurities regarding being the topic of town gossip. He didn't want to ruin her festive mood.

Kit slowed down as they approached a table set up by a new toy store in town. Her eyes widened and she let out a gasp. She picked up a purple ukulele and began gently strumming it.

"This is beautiful. The artistry is incredible," Kit said, admiring the instrument. "But Ada's a little young for it. Maybe in a few years."

"What about the chocolate teddy bear or the hand puppets?" Leo asked, after scouring the items on display.

Kit picked up two vibrantly colored cloth puppets and began playing with them. She was having so much fun with the toys, showing that she was a kid at heart herself.

"This is perfect for her. I can tell her stories and use the puppets as a visual." She dug into her purse and pulled out some cash. "I'd like to buy these two please and the ukulele as well," she said to the vendor with a satisfied smile. She turned toward Leo. "My brother will get a kick out of the ukulele." Within minutes, the items were purchased and bagged up. Kit's expression was one of pure happiness. Clearly, it gave her immense joy picking special gifts for her family.

The next stop was the cotton candy stand for Leo. Normally he didn't have much of a sweet tooth, but the sticky confection was his absolute favorite. He found it impossible to resist. As soon as the cotton candy hit his tongue, Leo groaned.

"That good, huh?" Kit asked with a chuckle, her eyes glued to him.

"See for yourself," he said, tearing off a piece and offering it to her. "Open your mouth," he instructed before placing it on her tongue.

"Oh, wow," she exclaimed, closing her eyes. "It's way better than I remember. This takes me back to when we were kids. There was always cotton candy at the school carnival. I remember one year I ate so much of it I got a bellyache."

Leo frowned. "Now that I think about it, eating too much of this stuff always gives me a bellyache."

"Maybe you need some real food such as protein or soup or French fries," Kit said.

"If you're hungry we can go to the Snowy Owl," Leo suggested. "The food is fantastic and it's a good place to people watch."

"Great idea," Kit said. As they headed over to the diner, Leo knew with a deep certainty that they were the topic of conversation. He wasn't going to let a few whispers stop him from enjoying Kit's company. For too long now he'd sequestered himself at the farm, submerged in grief. From now on, he was only taking forward steps. Life was way too short to block the blessings that were all around him.

Once they stepped inside the Snowy Owl Diner, delectable aromas permeated the air. She looked around, noting the plush leather booths, the colorful jukebox and the festive holiday decorations—more bling than the last time she'd been in here. Holly hung above every booth and a fully decorated Christmas tree sat in the corner. Owl Creek sure loved decking the halls! It was so nice to raise her daughter in a quaint town that saw the beauty in Christmas and spreading cheer.

Braden North, Piper's husband, greeted Leo with a slap on the back. "Hey there, guys. Thanks for stopping in. Are you taking a break from the festivities?"

"Hi, Braden. We figured that we needed some sustenance. The treats at the event are amazing, but too much of a good thing if you know what I mean," Leo explained.

"Seems we're not the only ones," Kit said, looking around the crowded diner.

Braden nodded. "We've been super busy. I've been holding down the fort while Piper is selling the pies, but she should be back soon." He let out a chuckle. "I can't tell you how many we baked for this event. When

I close my eyes at night, I'm going to have visions of rhubarb pies dancing in my head."

Leo and Kit both chuckled at the visual. Clearly, Pie in the Sky kept Piper and Braden busy. The business had been a huge boon for the diner's income, so Kit knew Piper deeply appreciated Owl Creek's support.

"Well, let me get you guys into a booth so you can eat before the tree lighting starts," Braden said as he picked up two menus and led them to a booth table. "We'll be closing up the diner early so we can make it to the ceremony for Ethan."

Kit scooted into the booth across from Leo and glanced over the menu.

"I appreciate that, buddy," Leo said. "And I know Aunt Ivy and Uncle Jamie will as well."

"Of course," Braden said. "Ethan wasn't just a friend, he was a role model. The way he lived his life taught me a lot about being honorable."

"He showed us all about courage," Leo said, his expression solemn.

Kit sensed Leo was still in the grip of grief. It was understandable. He and his cousin had been close and he'd left this world way too soon. For Kit, it still felt surreal knowing that Ethan had given her the greatest gift of all—Ada. She would always remember him fondly.

A grin broke out over Braden's face as he looked over at the diner's entrance. "Piper's back. I'll send a server over to take your order," Braden said before walking off to greet his wife.

A few minutes later, a waitress came over with waters, then took their orders with Kit selecting the haddock and chips, while Leo picked the salmon chowder and a turkey club sandwich.

She locked eyes with him from across the table "So, how are you dealing with the holidays so far?" she asked, hoping she wasn't crossing any lines. "I know it must be difficult grappling with loss during the happiest time of the year."

"I appreciate you asking. People tend not to inquire. Maybe it's awkward or they think it's a sensitive topic when in fact it makes me feel seen, as if my grief is being acknowledged."

She reached across the table and placed her hand over his. "I understand. You want your loved ones to be remembered. And mourned. If it helps to know, I always hear people talking about your dad and Ethan. About what a huge loss it was to Owl Creek to lose both of them." She took a sip of her water. "I think it says a lot that they were so beloved."

"It does. Every time someone shares a story about them, it lifts me up. For a long time, it was salt in the wound, but I've turned a corner," Leo explained. "You helped me realize that I can't shrink away from honoring and talking about my loved ones."

"Blessed are they that mourn, for they shall be comforted." The words slipped out of her mouth. It struck her as something Leo might need to hear right about now.

"One of my favorite verses," Leo said with a nod of his head. "I've read that passage from Matthew countless times in the last year."

"I hope it's been inspirational for you." Leo deserved to be at peace.

"It really has. What I'm learning is that no man is an island, even in grief." He leaned forward across the table. "Training with you and Jupiter, as well as the rest of the group, has given me a purpose. And being here at today's celebration reminded me about the ties that bind us as community. Even in my darkest hour, I'm not alone."

That resonated with her on a deep level. She and Leo were walking different paths, but they were both dealing with loss. And like Leo, she was realizing that she wasn't going to be alone on her journey.

The jukebox suddenly began blaring an up-tempo holiday tune. The beats of "Rockin' Around the Christmas Tree" filled the establishment. Invigorated by the music, Kit began tapping her fingers on the table. Leo began to hum along with the song, his expression animated as he started singing the lyrics.

Just then the waitress returned to their table and placed their meals down in front of them. They began to eat with gusto, relishing the delicious food. Once they couldn't eat a bite more, they paid the tab and said their goodbyes to Braden, who was sitting at the counter with Piper.

"Look! They're standing right under the mistletoe!" A small child cried out, pointing at Leo and Kit.

Leo looked up and let out a groan. "Uh-oh. We fell right into the trap."

"Oh, no," Kit said as her eyes followed his gaze to the sprig of mistletoe hanging directly above them.

How many times had she witnessed other people getting caught unaware standing under the diner's legendary Christmas mistletoe?

"Yep, we're standing right under the mistletoe," Leo whispered. His features were slightly pinched. "Should we make a run for it? Get out of Dodge?"

"I don't want to run away. It *is* a diner tradition," Kit conceded. She couldn't remember a time when diners hadn't kissed under this particular mistletoe. Kit had a vivid memory of her own parents kissing in this very spot, spurred on by Kit and her siblings.

"It would be strange if we didn't. Right?" Leo asked.

Kit chewed on the inside of her cheek. It would look churlish if they didn't go along with it. Kit hadn't ever seen anyone refuse. Maybe they should just quickly kiss and move past this awkward moment.

"What are you waiting for?" Braden asked with a smirk from the sidelines.

"Kiss her, Leo," Piper prodded as the other diners took up the chant for them to kiss.

"All right. Take it easy," Leo said, glaring at Braden, who was wiggling his eyebrows in their direction.

Kit turned her face up to Leo moments before he dipped his head down and placed his mouth over hers. *On the lips?* She'd been expecting a peck on the cheek. For a moment, time seemed to stand still as his lips tenderly caressed her own. The kiss didn't last for long, but it was time enough for Kit to realize how much she liked being kissed by Leo. His lips were soft and tender. The woodsy scent of him rose to her nostrils. Leo stepped away from her and she heard loud applause surrounding them. She could feel her cheeks getting flushed and she wasn't sure if it was a direct result of the gawking diners or the dazzling kiss.

In the moment, Kit had wanted it to go on and on. She'd been completely and utterly swept away.

"Let's get out of here," Leo said, grabbing her hand and tugging her out the door to sounds of lighthearted laughter. Neither one said a word as they walked back toward the festivities. Had Leo felt the same way as she did about their mistletoe kiss? Or had he simply been going through the motions? All she could think about was kissing him again. Hopefully, without a crowd watching their every move.

Just as they reached the edge of the town green, the decorations on the Christmas tree came to life with hundreds of twinkling, dazzling lights glowing like beacons. A gold star glinted from on top of the tree. They edged closer and watched as kids gathered around it, letting out excited squeals. Seeing the tree lighting through a child's eyes was wonderful. Kit couldn't wait until Adaline was old enough to enjoy the town tradition. A group of Christmas carolers began singing "Mary, Did You Know?" in front of the tree.

It was so moving tears sprung to her eyes. She could feel Leo's eyes on her. "This was always my favorite part of Christmas. The carolers. I used to love when they went door to door."

"I remember that. It's pretty rare to see them doing that these days," Leo noted.

"It's always such a treat." Maybe next year Kit would

join the carolers. She prayed that things would be going well for her a year from now.

"They're about to start the ceremony for Ethan," Leo said in a somber voice. "I want to make sure I'm standing at the front with my family."

Kit froze upon hearing Leo's comment. Today had been a wonderful day, filled with fun and festivity. Now, she'd been jolted back into reality. *Ethan.* How could she stand next to Leo and listen to Ethan being honored by the town without bursting into tears? The heroic man being lauded by her hometown was Adaline's father, one her daughter would never know due to a cruel twist of fate. She followed numbly behind Leo, taking little breaths to ease the panic threatening to overtake her. A crush of people cut her off from Leo so that he was far ahead of her in the crowd moving toward the stage. He didn't even realize that she wasn't right behind him. Kit made a split-second decision that caused her to turn around and head in the opposite direction as fast as her legs could carry her.

Once she made her way back to the shop, Kit let herself in and sank down onto a comfy chair. Her hands were shaking and her legs felt wobbly. She couldn't go on like this much longer. She was spending so much time with Leo and growing closer to him each and every day. They'd kissed earlier, and even though it had been a bit forced by the hanging mistletoe, Kit had felt sparks between them.

One way or the other, Kit needed to find a way to tell Leo and his family the truth before it blew up in her face.

* * *

What had happened to Kit?

One moment she'd been standing right beside him, while in the very next she'd vanished into thin air. Leo looked in all directions to see if he could spot her, but for all intents and purposes she was gone. The area was congested, so it wouldn't be surprising if she'd lost sight of him in the crowd. He was kicking himself for not grabbing a hold of her hand to make sure they remained together. With her vision issues, she might not be able to see him in a crowded area.

Leo couldn't help but worry about Kit. Had she received a call about Ada and left? Was something wrong? Leo had really wanted Kit beside him during the tribute to his cousin. Today had cemented how much he enjoyed spending time with her. More and more, Kit was becoming an integral part of his life.

Leo moved up front to stand with his family. He reached out and put his arm around Aunt Ivy's shoulder. She leaned in and pressed her head against his chest. Her shoulders were shaking. Uncle Patrick stood on the other side of Uncle Jamie, tightly gripping his hand. Florence, the twins, his mother and Aunt Renata huddled together.

Beulah, now dressed in her signature peacock blue coat and pearls, stood on the makeshift stage and spoke into the microphone. "We gathered today for our annual holiday stroll, an event that allows us to celebrate Christmas and promote local businesses. We pause to remember one of our own, Ethan Duggan. Ethan was many things to the town of Owl Creek. Beloved son.

Nephew. Cousin. Scholar. Athlete. Most of all, he was a man of faith. He died heroically in the service of this country. It is with pleasure and a deep sense of gratitude that we present this plaque to the parents of Ethan Duggan, who will forever remain in our hearts and minds. He leaves behind a legacy of heroism and sacrifice. A true Alaskan hero."

As the crowd clapped enthusiastically, Aunt Ivy and Uncle Jamie headed to the platform to accept the plaque in Ethan's honor. A fierce sense of pride spread through Leo's chest. Ethan had always excelled at making his family proud and this occasion was no different. As the ceremony concluded, Leo began scanning the crowd for any sign of Kit. He still had no idea where she'd disappeared to. Had she left the event without saying goodbye?

"Looking for Kit?" his mother asked. A quick look in her direction showed a smile twitching at the sides of her lips.

Leo shrugged. "She did a disappearing act." They'd been having such a good time. Or had they? Perhaps he shouldn't have kissed her. Even though it began as a lark, the kiss had morphed into something rash and foolish, crossing so many lines that shouldn't have been breached. In the moment, it had felt sensational, but now he was filled with regret. And clearly Kit was also, he thought with a snort. She'd left without a word of goodbye. Kit had bailed on him during an emotional moment for him and his family.

"If you want an unsolicited opinion," she said, arching her eyebrows, "I think the two of you make a fantastic pair."

"We're not a couple, Mama. Kit's my friend. End of story." In a perfect world, perhaps they could be more, but he wasn't ready to lay his heart on the line again. Not even for Kit. The risk was far too great. And why jeopardize a friendship by crossing lines in the sand?

"Leo, I know it's none of my business, but you need love in your life. You can't let one bad experience hold you back." His mother's voice bordered on pleading.

Bad experience? How had his mother known about his heartbreak? The only person he'd confided in was Ace. He turned toward her, studying her expression. "What do you know about that?"

She narrowed her gaze as she regarded him. "I'm your mother, Leo. I know when you're hurting. I saw the sadness in your eyes that only a broken heart can cause."

He leaned in and kissed her on the cheek. "Mama, I'm fine. If it's meant to be, love is going to find me."

She held out her arm. "You just gave me goose bumps, son. No one deserves it more than you. Just keep your heart open and it will come."

Leo didn't bother to tell her that he didn't really believe in love. He knew without a doubt that hearing those words from his lips would break his mother's heart.

The tightening sensation on the back of his neck wouldn't ease up. He couldn't shake this unsettled feeling about Kit. Was she all right? He sensed that although she put on a brave face, she was troubled about the future. Leo wanted everything in Kit's life to be settled. Every night he prayed her vision loss wouldn't be catastrophic and that some of her sight would remain intact. He ached to take her in his arms and tell her that everything was going to be all right, but he knew it would be taking their relationship a step too far. She was his friend and nothing more. The thought of going any further and getting his heart broken again was a huge deterrent.

Then why had he kissed her earlier? It hadn't been a simple kiss either. Leo couldn't stop reliving it in his mind. It had been full of tenderness and longing. The best kiss of his life!

Leo would be lying to himself if he didn't acknowledge that he had doubts about Kit. She'd never spoken much about Adaline's father, which continued to be a huge red flag. All Kit had told him was that he would never be a part of Ada's life. He ran a shaky hand over his face as he headed to his truck. But it was too late to distance himself from her. She'd gotten under his skin and burrowed inside.

The thought of getting burned again terrified him. How had he let this happen?

Chapter Twelve

Kit arrived at the Duggan ranch before sunrise. The sky was a beautiful color as the sun slowly crept over the horizon. She was eager to get back to her training with Jupiter. And Leo. She couldn't deny how the sight of him caused her pulse to skitter.

When she opened the barn door, she paused for a moment to admire Leo before he was aware of her presence. Dressed in a hunter green parka and a pair of dark cords, Leo looked stylish and rugged. His head was down so she couldn't see his lovely hazel eyes. She'd never seen anyone with eyes like Leo's. They seemed to look straight inside her, all the way down to the secrets she was keeping.

Jupiter let out a cry and came running toward her. Kit immediately began giving him commands, which he quickly performed. "That's a good boy," Kit crooned, patting the top of the dog's head. She was so incredibly fortunate to have Jupiter, whose main job in the future would be to keep her safe and on course. Every time she thought about stumbling or falling, she thought about Jupiter's role in her life. He would help her stay steady. Leo swung his gaze toward her, gifting her with a brilliant smile.

A squeezing sensation in her chest felt slightly alarming. She had never felt like this in the presence of a man before. Not even Ethan.

"Hey there," Leo said. "I was worried about you the other night when I couldn't find you."

"I texted you after I left," she said sheepishly. "I needed to get home to Ada. Sorry if you were concerned about me."

"Thanks. I didn't see your message until I got home, but it was nice of you to let me know what happened."

"I heard Ethan's ceremony was touching." Jules had stuck around to attend the tribute, then reported back to her later on. Kit had felt ashamed about running off. Now she wouldn't be able to tell her daughter about how the town honored her father.

"It was," Leo said. "I wish you could've been there. Aunt Ivy and Uncle Jamie were incredibly moved by the tribute. His legacy will live on through his incredible service to this country and those who love him."

Suddenly Kit's throat felt as dry as sandpaper. Ethan did have a part of him that lived on. Ada. She opened her mouth to confess everything to Leo, but the words were lodged behind a wall of fear. How could she convey all the reasons why she'd handled things so poorly?

"We're going to do some obstacle training today. I think that will be beneficial for both of you since it will be important for him to alert you to items in your path. Jupiter's a little bit ahead of the curve, so I'm curious to see if he keeps up the pace."

"Sounds good to me," Kit said, ready to dig in to make up for the lesson she'd bailed on.

For the next hour and a half, they put Jupiter through his paces. When Leo called for a break, Kit provided Jupiter with a few snacks and some water as they stepped outside the barn. A cold wind swept across Kit's face, but after training in the heated barn, it was refreshing.

"Good job, Jupiter. You deserve a break." He grinned at the guide dog in training. "And you too, Kit. He definitely knows you're his person. So we're going to do public access in the next few weeks. That will entail us going into town, which could provide a nice change of scenery for the training."

"That's exciting, but I love doing our lessons out here at the ranch. I think you have one of the most spectacular views in all of Owl Creek." She looked out at the glorious snow-capped mountains and the wide expanse of pristine land owned by Leo's family. Waking up to this incredible vista every day must be a blessing.

"I appreciate the foresight of my ancestors. They wanted this ranch to carry on from generation to generation. So Florence's kids will take up the reins one day. My sister's as well."

"And yours," she added. An image of two sandy-haired boys that looked like Leo flashed before her eyes. *What was wrong with her?* If she weren't careful, she was going to start imagining herself as Leo's future wife. A sigh slipped past her lips. She used to dream a lot about happily-ever-afters. When had she stopped fantasizing about finding a forever type of love? Perhaps there was a part of her that no longer felt worthy of it after her fling with Ethan and getting pregnant with Ada. It was pretty rare for unwed mothers to be the princess in a fairy tale.

Leo shrugged. "I've always wanted kids…at least two. But I'm not sure it'll ever happen."

"So, why are you still single?" Kit asked. She'd wondered for a while now how a keeper like Leo wasn't taken. What woman wouldn't want to be Leo's other half? He was strong, dependable and kind. If her situation were different, Kit wouldn't have a single reservation about being with Leo. But it would be hard to build something meaningful without telling him her truths. The very thought of doing so caused her a great deal of anxiety.

Leo shifted from one foot to the other. He couldn't hide his discomfort. It radiated from him in waves. "I don't know exactly. I thought once…not too long ago that I'd found my person, my other half." He let out a ragged puff of air. Pain was etched on his face.

"What happened?" she asked. "If I may ask."

He focused on a spot in the distance, then cleared his throat. "This is tough to talk about," he said, clenching his jaw. "I met a woman named Dahlia at a horse auction in Fairbanks. She was from Palmer where her family owned a small ranch. We hit it off from the start. I fell for her pretty fast. We exchanged texts and phone calls. We even chatted online, which isn't my favorite thing, but I wanted our relationship to blossom so I participated. I even gave her money to pay some bills and buy a used car so she could get to her job. Sadly, she was all smoke and mirrors. She made me think that she had feelings for me, but in the end, I was just being used for what I could give her."

"Oh, no, Leo. That's terrible." It was horrible that someone had so cruelly tricked him. Shame was laced into his tone. She sensed his deep embarrassment and her heart ached for him. All his losses had piled up, one after the other, burying him underneath the rubble.

"That's not the worst of it," he admitted, breaking eye contact with her.

She waited for him to explain, knowing he might need some time to get the words out.

"The day my father had his attack, I wasn't here at the ranch because I was meeting up with Dahlia." His face crumpled. "I had sent her money to fly to Owl Creek so we could continue our relationship. I figured I'd show her my world here at the ranch. Only thing was she never showed up." Leo's voice thickened with emotion. "By the time I got back home, my father had suffered a fatal attack. And days later, I reached out to Dahlia to tell her about my dad, but she wouldn't take my calls. When she finally did, she broke things off. She was so cold and unfeeling, Kit. And I have no one to blame but myself for being such a colossal fool and for thinking she cared about me."

"Leo! Please don't say those things about yourself," Kit scolded him. "It's not your fault someone decided to do such a cruel thing to you. That's not on you. That's between them and God. There's something courageous about seeking out love, whether it's long-distance or in person."

"But don't you see, Kit?" he asked, his eyes beseeching her to understand. "If I hadn't been such an idiot, I would have been here to help my father. I may have been able to save him."

"And there's a chance that even if you had been there, he would still have slipped away. Truly, only God holds that answer," Kit said. "With time, I pray your guilt turns into acceptance that sometimes bad things happen and we're powerless to change them. It's something I'm learning to accept in my own life."

"I like the way you cling to your faith, Kit. You have a way about you that makes me want to share things with you. So far I've only talked about this with Ace." His eyes radiated gratitude. "You're easy to talk to."

Kit wasn't certain, but she felt as if her smile was stretching from ear to ear. "I feel the same way about you."

"It's really hard not to beat myself up over what happened. A year later and I still feel like such a fool," he admitted.

She let out a surprised sound. "That's the last way I'd ever describe you. From where I'm standing, Leo Duggan, you're wonderful."

For a few moments, their words sat between them like a warm caress.

Kit was looking up at him as snowflakes swirled all around them. A few dotted the bridge of her nose and cheeks. He couldn't take his eyes off her. Even though

Leo knew that kissing Kit should be the last thing on his agenda, he couldn't drag his eyes away from her full rosy lips. This woman was beautiful in every way imaginable. Inside and out. Upside down and sideways.

"Kit," he said in a low voice as he placed her face between his gloved hands. At the moment, there wasn't a single force in this world that could have stopped him from kissing her. She moved closer toward him so that there wasn't any space between them.

"Yes, please," she murmured, closing her eyes as he lowered his mouth to hers. Leo was prepared to take his time with this kiss. He would savor every second of it. A sweet floral scent filled his nostrils. It was the same aroma that always hovered around Kit. Her lips were soft and inviting. He felt her hands gripping the collar of his jacket, pulling him ever closer. The kiss soared and deepened, with Kit kissing him back with equal intensity. As far as kisses went, Leo knew this one was special. He was tempted to keep kissing her until they needed to come up for air.

As the kiss ended, neither one pulled away from their close proximity. He could hear her heart thumping against his chest. He leaned his head down so their foreheads rested against one another's.

"That was...pretty amazing," Kit said, sounding breathless.

And long overdue, Leo thought. This was different from the mistletoe kiss. Although it had been enjoyable, they'd been forced into it by the mistletoe. This one was pure yearning come to fruition.

He'd wanted to kiss Kit ever since they were teenagers. Back then it had been about crushing on her. Now, it was about their connection. The attraction that hung in the air between them whenever they were near one another.

At the moment, her eyes were shining brightly, her cheeks flushed with color.

"I've been wanting to do that for a while now," Leo admitted. "But at the same time I didn't want to blow up our friendship."

His reservations were valid.

Even though Kit seemed like the woman of his dreams, Leo knew she was keeping secrets. They'd gotten incredibly close over the last few weeks and even though he had confided in her about his heartbreaking experience with Dahlia, she still hadn't told him about Adaline's father. It bothered him as a man who'd previously been caught up in a deception. A part of him believed it wasn't any of his business, but it was hard to fathom why it was such a deeply buried secret. Why wasn't this mystery man in Ada's life? Who was he?

Her lack of transparency caused his imagination to run wild. Had Kit been involved with a married man? Someone in jail? Ugh. He hated himself for even going down that road with his thoughts, but it was impossible for his mind not to go there.

"I get it," Kit said. "But I'll always value our friendship, no matter what. You've done so much for me. A kiss can't change that."

"No, it can't," Leo said, praying Kit was right. She was one of the most important people in his life, and he couldn't imagine his life without her plucky, determined spirit.

But what if he was falling for her? These feelings he was grappling with felt way more intense than friendship. His head was telling him to tread lightly, while his heart urged him to take a chance.

Believe! Wasn't that a big part of Christmas? His faith told him to believe on a regular basis and he'd always held on, even in the darkest of times.

"We're having a Christmas Eve party at the ranch. Not a big blowout or anything," Leo told Kit with a chuckle after they concluded their training for the day. "Just a small gathering of friends and family in order to celebrate the holidays. Would you like to come as my guest? You and Ada, of course."

Ada. She loved that he'd included her daughter in the invite. It made her happy to know that Leo saw Adaline as an extension of Kit. Her little girl meant the world to her. If she and Leo could explore a relationship, Ada would factor into the equation. Leo was tacitly acknowledging that reality. For just a moment, she allowed herself to imagine how wonderful that would be. Unfortunately, Kit knew it wasn't possible for them to be together, even if Leo didn't.

Kit hesitated to accept. She would adore spending Christmas Eve with the Duggans. But, on the other hand, it would be placing Adaline right under their noses. That didn't feel right to her. Perhaps it was her guilty conscience rearing up to put a wrinkle in a sweet invitation.

Perhaps she needed to keep a wall up between her and Leo since the truth about Ethan being Ada's father felt like a ticking time bomb. But she really wanted to say yes! Celebrating at the Double D Ranch with Leo and his family would be lovely. They would make memories to last a lifetime. That's what she wanted more than anything, even though she knew it wasn't a wise choice.

"I would really like that," Kit said, giving in on impulse to the invite. Spending a festive evening with Leo was simply too tempting to turn down. She couldn't recall the last time she had been invited to a party. Once she'd gotten pregnant with Adaline, her limited social life had dried up. Would it be so wrong to enjoy herself in a festive setting during this blessed time of the year?

"Great. I'll see you then," Leo said, seemingly pleased by her response. "By the way, we have a fun game we play called Alaskan Swap. If you want to play along, bring a wrapped inexpensive gift…trash or treasure. It's your decision. Then we all pick from the pile and swap or steal from someone else."

Kit chuckled. "It sounds fun." She imagined it got pretty lively with all the swapping and swiping of presents. She pictured herself sitting in the Duggans' living room with Ada perched on her lap as the Duggan family played their festive Christmas game.

As Kit drove away from the ranch, thoughts of their tender kiss came into sharp focus. She couldn't stop reliving it in her mind. She hadn't been kissed many times in her twenty-seven years, but this had been one for the ages. Kit wondered what it would be like to walk through life with a man like Leo. To be on the receiving end of his endless kisses and his nurturing spirit.

She let out a frustrated sound. Why was her mind even going there? She'd given in to her desire to share a kiss with Leo. In the moment, it had been incredibly romantic and swoon-worthy, but upon closer inspection it just seemed reckless. *The heart wants what the heart wants.* The expression popped into her head, reminding her that her actions weren't always based on reason.

Leo consistently made her feel special and cherished. He evoked emotions in her she'd never before experienced. And it terrified her. Kit knew she was placing her hand too close to the fire. Leo wasn't an option for her. Eventually the truth about Ethan being Adaline's father would come out. It was inevitable. And when that happened, Leo wouldn't be inviting her to any more family events or kissing her tenderly.

Everything seemed to be coming together in her life with her career and her training with Jupiter, yet at the same time Kit felt as if she were standing on a precipice. One wrong move and she would plummet over the edge. With a gnawing sensation in her belly, Kit realized that she was falling for Leo. In a perfect world, this realization would be a feel-good moment, but she felt sick to her stomach. Leo Duggan was the very last man she should be developing feelings for. What she felt for Leo would only amount to heartache.

Kit let herself in the back entrance of the shop, pausing along the way to grab a few items that she'd purchased from an estate sale in Homer. She loved buying vintage items and then filling up the shop with them.

Kit prayed her loss of vision wouldn't be so profound that she wouldn't be able to continue doing what she loved.

A few customers couldn't seem to take their eyes off her as she walked around the shop, putting new items on display. Kit knew that she wasn't being paranoid. They were alternating between stares and whispers. As soon as the two older women made their purchases and left the shop, Kit approached Jules.

"Was I just imagining getting the stink eye from Helen and Rosanne?" Kit asked as soon as the women left the shop. She was baffled by their behavior. It had been a long time since she was the object of such looks—most of which happened during her pregnancy—but this was bringing up all those awful memories.

Jules's eyes bulged. She opened her mouth but no words came out.

"What's going on?" Kit asked. "You look shaken."

"Kit, you need to sit down," Jules instructed, leading her over to a comfy velour chair.

"Why? What's happened?" Kit asked, sinking down onto the seat. Fear made her legs wobbly. "Did something happen to Adaline?" *Dear Lord, please let Ada be safe and secure. I don't know what I would do in this world without her.*

"Oh, no, Kit. Adaline is fine. I'm sorry for scaring you, but it's nothing like that," Jules explained. "There's a rumor going around about you and Leo."

Kit exhaled. She could handle a few whispers. Been there, done that. And she'd survived. "Is that it? I can't really be upset. We were seen together at the holiday stroll and we kissed under the mistletoe at the Snowy Owl."

Jules made a tutting sound. "That's not the whole of it." Her sister began nibbling at her fingernails.

"Tell me," she begged. "This must be bad."

"Oh, Kit. I'm so sorry. They're saying that Leo is Adaline's father."

Chapter Thirteen

All was right in his world, Leo thought. Finally, he felt as if he were on solid ground. Ever since Kit had left, he'd been singing an upbeat Christmas tune and thinking about his future. For the first time in forever, Leo was feeling hopeful about the days and months stretched out before him. And it was all because of Kit. Sweet, plucky Kit, who had more courage than anyone he'd ever known.

His thoughts of Kit were interrupted by the sound of tires making a crackling sound as a vehicle pulled up a few feet away from him. He would recognize the dog rescue van from a mile away. Ace's work mobile was white with a big canine logo on the side. Ace enjoyed advertising his dog rescue all over Owl Creek. Leo ambled over to the van and greeted Ace as soon as he stepped out of the vehicle.

"Hey, Ace. I wasn't expecting to see you, even though you keep promising to swing by to check in on Daisy and Jupiter."

"Can you blame me?" he asked with a full-throated chuckle. "I'm up to my ears in pups at the Owl Creek dog rescue. I can barely get a moment to myself."

"You love it though," Leo said, recognizing the look of contentment etched on his friend's face. What a difference from last spring when Ace's life had been derailed by a sled racing accident. Finding love a second time around with his ex, Maya, had transformed him into a new man.

"Guilty as charged," Ace drawled. "What can I say? Dogs are in my blood."

As a former champion sled dog racer, Ace had spent the better part of his life surrounded by Siberian huskies and malamutes. Ace's family had been involved in the sport for generations, so he wasn't kidding about it being in his DNA.

Leo called out to Daisy and Jupiter, who quickly came running out of the barn.

Ace got down on his haunches and lavished both dogs with affection. "I can't believe how much they've both grown. You've done a great job, Leo. Maya saved their lives and you gave them a home." Ace's voice was husky with emotion.

"Are you getting soft on me?" Leo asked in a teasing tone.

Ace laughed out loud. "If I am, you can blame it on Maya. She likes my tender side."

Ace shoved his hands in the front pocket of his jeans. "So, I didn't just come by to see the dogs. There's something I heard in town that you need to know about."

"Okay, I think that I know where this is going. Is it

about me and Kit kissing at the diner?" Leo had known it wouldn't be long before tongues were wagging about their mistletoe kiss. He let out a snort. "I'm surprised it took so long."

Ace frowned. "This is about way more than a kiss. Somehow people have gotten it twisted. Folks are speculating that you're the father of Kit's little girl."

Leo sputtered. "W-What? Please tell me you're joking."

Ace shook his head. "You know that's not my style. There's nothing humorous about spreading lies."

Leo muttered under his breath. "I can't believe people would stoop so low. Kit and I have been spending a lot of time together recently, so I expected a few whispers, but to drag Ada into it is awful."

"Sorry, man. I thought you needed to know what's being said. Someone passed the rumor along to Maya at the clinic and she gave them a tongue-lashing."

"That's nice to hear," Leo said, thankful for Maya's support. "To be honest, it's such a ridiculous rumor that I can't believe anyone even passed it on." He ran his hand over his face. "I don't want my mother to hear it though. It might upset her. And Kit will be beside herself. I really should give her a call."

"So what's going on with you two?" Ace asked. "I asked you this before, but are you an item?"

"We seem to be moving in that direction," Leo conceded. "If it were up to me, I'd say yes."

"You seem really happy other than this stupid rumor," Ace said. "Don't let the gossip get you down.

It'll dissipate in a few days when they find another topic to jaw about."

"Oh, no. That looks like Kit's truck," Leo said as he noticed the tomato-colored vehicle barreling down the snow-covered lane.

"Are you two training today?" Ace asked, his gaze swinging toward the road as the vehicle turned to park by the barn.

"No," he said as he waited for her to emerge. "And that's what worries me. Kit wouldn't just show up here out of the blue. Unless—"

Ace raised an eyebrow. "Unless she's heard the rumors."

Leo nodded. "That's exactly what I'm thinking."

"I think that I should head out so the two of you can talk," Ace said, reaching out and clapping his best friend on the shoulder. "Don't worry too much. This too shall pass."

As Ace walked away, he crossed paths with Kit. They exchanged pleasantries before parting ways. Leo knew before Kit reached his side that she had heard the gossip about him and Ada. She seemed distraught. Leo considered it his job to soothe her soul.

"Leo, I'm sorry to just show up like this," Kit apologized, "but I need to talk to you."

"Hey there. Kit, you're welcome at the ranch anytime. You don't need a reason to swing by." He wanted her to feel comfortable here, as if she belonged. Leo hoped she would become a permanent fixture at the ranch.

"I appreciate you saying so," she said, offering him a

feeble smile. "Can we talk in private?" She cast a look around them. A few ranch hands were working in the stables, while others were out in the pasture. It seemed unlikely to Leo that they could overhear their conversation, but he wanted to put Kit at ease.

"Let's head into the barn. We can talk there," Leo suggested, walking in lockstep with Kit before holding the barn door open for her. Once they were inside, Leo knew he wouldn't hesitate to let Kit know he knew what she was upset about. More than anything he wanted to keep her calm and help her to understand that a thousand rumors about them couldn't change how he felt about her.

Without even realizing it until this very moment, Leo knew he was over the moon about Kit. He wanted things with her that he'd believed were no longer possible. Maybe he was getting ahead of himself, but it was how he felt. It was stunning, considering how he'd vowed to keep his heart on ice. Kit had thawed out his soul, to the point where he was able to believe once more in the possibility of loving again.

He was just going to be direct with Kit instead of avoiding the subject. "Ace told me about the ridiculous rumor flying around. I have a feeling that's why you came over. Am I right?" he asked.

She nodded, blinking back tears. A few ran down her cheeks and he reached out and brushed them away with his thumb.

"Please don't cry, Kit. I can't stand to see you so unhappy. This foolishness isn't worth it."

"I never wanted you to be dragged into my mess," she said, letting out a wail.

He dipped his head down and brushed his lips against her temple. "I'm not worried one little bit about foul rumors. We know the truth. That's all that matters."

Kit pressed her hands against his chest and gently pushed him away. She looked up at him with anguish emanating from her eyes. "No, Leo. You don't know the truth. And it's high time you did."

Kit breathed in deeply through her nostrils. There was nothing to do at this point but be honest with Leo. Things had already gone too far with people gossiping that he was her baby's father. It was incredibly unfair to drag Leo into her personal business. He didn't deserve to be whispered about or pointed a finger at. She knew from her own experiences how painful it could be and she couldn't bear to see him treated this way. It could negatively affect him in ways he didn't fully understand. This moment had been building ever since the day she had discovered that she was carrying Ethan's child. Not telling the truth had created ripples throughout the lives of others.

Dear Lord, please let my decision to tell the truth serve as a healing balm for all of us. Adaline deserves to know the identity of her father and to be embraced by the Duggan family. Adaline's future hung in the balance. Kit cared so deeply for Leo. She needed him to understand that her actions had arisen out of fear and shame. She had never meant to lie to him. *In order to achieve redemption, I need the truth to shine like the brightest of stars.*

"What do you mean?" Leo asked with a frown.

He looked totally baffled. It wrecked her to know that she was about to pull the rug from underneath him. He wouldn't even see it coming. She swallowed past her fear. Kit needed to rip the Band-Aid off rather than continue with her deception. Anything less would be cruel.

"Leo, I've been wanting to tell you this for such a long time," she said, wringing her hands. "For so many weeks and months, I didn't know what to do. Or how to say it." She forced herself to meet his gaze. His beautiful hazel eyes radiated confusion.

"You can tell me anything. I hope you know that," he said, his voice sounding like a warm caress.

"Have you ever felt completely alone? So lost you thought that you might never find a way out of the darkness?" she asked him. Suddenly, it felt as if she were reliving the nightmare. This moment was as equally devastating as the turbulent times she'd endured. She feared nothing in her life would ever be the same again.

"You know I've been there. I told you all about it. Losing Ethan, then my dad. Being played for a fool by Dahlia. I've experienced what you're describing."

"You did," she said in a soft voice. "And I'm so sorry you went through all of that."

"Kit, what is this all about? You can talk to me. I'm here for you."

"This rumor about you being Ada's father hit me pretty hard."

He reached out and smoothed a few stray strands of hair away from her face. "You can't let something like that rattle you. Just put it out of your mind. I promise you I'm not dwelling on it."

"I can't shove it under a rug. Not this time." She bowed her head as shame threatened to consume her. "It hits too close to the truth. Leo, Ada's father is Ethan."

A strangled sound came out of Leo's mouth. Disbelief was etched on his face. "No, that can't be right," he said, shaking his head vigorously. "Why are you saying this? It's not possible."

"It's the truth," she said, looking straight into his eyes. "And I know that I should have told Ethan's parents a long time ago, but I wasn't strong enough. I failed to do what was right."

For a moment, her confession sat in the air around them like a detonated bomb.

"Did Ethan know?" he asked in a raspy voice.

"No, he didn't. I waited too late…and then he was gone. I'll regret it for the rest of my life," she admitted. Maybe by introducing Ada to her grandparents she could somehow make up for it. She offered up that prayer from deep inside her.

Leo recoiled from her. "He never knew he was a father? Just like you never told Aunt Ivy and Uncle Jamie they had a grandbaby. How could you keep their grandchild away from them for all this time? They had every right to know!"

Kit wanted to run away from the anger she saw on

Leo's face, but she'd done enough hiding. She had to face what she'd done instead of burying her head in the sand. She needed to answer all his questions. After all this time, it was the least she could do.

"I was wrong. With all of it. I have every intention of allowing Ivy and Jamie into Ada's life. Ethan and I… We were just together that one time—"

Leo held up his hand, slicing it through the air. "I don't want to hear about that."

"I'm just trying to explain how everything got so complicated. We weren't a couple. We didn't date. We just leaned on each other that one time and I ended up getting pregnant with Adaline. I didn't even have a way to contact Ethan and then a few months later he was engaged. Everything was happening so fast. It was swirling all around me while I was doing my best to bring a healthy baby into the world and keep my head above water."

Leo folded his arms across his chest. "It seems to me that you had a choice. If you'd told Ethan, he would have supported you. He would have been able to bond with his daughter or at least gotten a chance to meet her." A tremor ran across his jaw. "We all would have been there for you."

Just hearing those words from Leo's lips made her want to cry. Things would have been so different if she had navigated the situation in a better way. But it was impossible to go back in time and fix it. She needed to focus on moving forward. "I believe that with all of my heart, but at the time it seemed so complicated and I was so full of shame about my choices. I hid my pregnancy for a long time and my parents still don't know Ethan is Ada's father. So telling your family about Ada after Ethan died seemed impossible."

He scowled at her. "My family has been mourning my cousin for well over a year. You could have eased some of the pain by telling us about Ethan's daughter. She's the most solid link to him. A piece of Ethan that will carry on despite the fact that he's no longer with us. Even though you're her mother, you had absolutely no right to withhold Ada from us." He was breathing heavily now and pacing back and forth. He shoved a hand through his hair and let out an agonized sound.

She agreed with him. Kit wasn't sure how she had ever thought her actions were acceptable. Fear had messed with her mindset. She'd dug herself a hole that she hadn't been able to escape from.

"Ada is my blessing in the storm," she said in a trembling voice. "I can't imagine my life without her. I know this is very overdue, but she'll be a godsend to your family as well."

"They're going to be shattered." Leo sunk his head into his hands. When he finally swung his head back up, his eyes glittered with fury. "*You're* going to have to face my family once I break the news to them. This is going to be a huge bombshell."

"I can tell them, Leo," Kit said. "It's the least thing I can do to make up for my silence."

His lip curled upward into a sneer. "No, you already had ample time to do so, yet you didn't." He took a few steps away from her and gestured toward the barn door. "You need to leave, Kit. I can barely stand to look at you."

"Leo, please. Let's talk through this. I know that I messed up. I don't want everything you and I have been building to be destroyed." She stepped toward him. "I care so much for you."

He shook his head. "How can I possibly believe that? If you had a single ounce of feeling for me, you would have told me the truth. Do you know how agonizing it feels to know I was deceived again by someone I care about so much? You just need to go. Leave."

There was no point in trying to get through to Leo at this point. He didn't want to hear a single thing she had to say about the two of them. It had all crashed and burned right before her eyes. Without saying another word, she began walking away from Leo, her heart breaking into little pieces with every step she took.

All her secrets had come tumbling out of the closet in one fell swoop. As a result, Leo wanted nothing more to do with her. The look of disgust on his face said it all. Jupiter began to trail behind her before she heard Leo's sharp command for the dog to stay.

Not only had she lost Leo, but it was likely that she'd forfeited her opportunity to work with Jupiter as well. It was heartbreaking.

As she stepped outside, the air whipped straight through her without Kit feeling a thing. She was numb with pain and there wasn't a single way to fix this mess she'd created. Everything she'd done had been in the best interest of Adaline, but in trying to protect her, she'd caused a world of pain for Leo and his family.

What if the Duggans hated her for what she'd done and turned Adaline against her? She'd already lost so much. It would be unbearable if her daughter was another casualty of her lies.

Chapter Fourteen

Leo sank down onto a bale of hay and covered his face with his hands. He felt Jupiter's presence beside him before the pup began to enthusiastically lick his hand. Leo wrapped his arms around the dog and pulled him close. "Thanks, Jupiter. I needed that."

Pain sliced through him, and it was way worse than before. This ache inside him made his past heartbreak feel like child's play. Once again, he'd been played for a fool. He felt as if he had been run over by a Mack truck he hadn't even seen coming. Had he been willfully blind?

Ada was a mini me of Ethan. She had the same brilliant blue eyes and hair color. The truth had been sitting under his nose this entire time. Why hadn't he figured it out on his own? If he had, he wouldn't be grappling with being sucker punched.

Leo waited until dinnertime to head up to the house. It had taken him hours to figure out how he was going to tell his family, particularly Uncle Jamie and Aunt

Ivy. How could he gently break the news that they had a grandbaby? He barely ate a bite of the meal his mother had so lovingly prepared.

As family dinner wound to a close, Leo made his announcement.

"I need to talk to everyone about something after dinner," Leo said. What was wrong with him? A huge lump of emotion sat in his throat. Would he even be able to get the words out about Ada? He looked over at Florence. "You might want to put the boys to bed first."

"Sure thing," Florence said, getting up from the table and collecting her plate along with the boys. "We're basically done so I'll come back downstairs after I tuck them in."

"Is everything okay, Leo?" his mother asked, reaching over and touching his hand.

"Not really, but it will be," he said with a nod. He prayed everything would come together for good once the truth was known by his family. Although this was a terrible situation, the one silver lining was Ada. Her presence in their lives would serve as a healing balm. Ethan was no longer with them, but Ada would serve as an extension of him. His best legacy.

With all eyes on him, Leo continued with his dinner as he practiced the words in his head. Once Florence returned and sat back down, Leo pushed his plate away and crossed his hands in front of him.

"Maybe you should have let us have dessert first," Jamie teased. "I hope this isn't the type of news that might make us lose our appetites."

"Do you ever lose yours?" Patrick asked, jabbing his brother in the side.

Uncle Jamie laughed. "What can I say? My wife likes a little extra padding around my middle."

Leo noticed Aunt Ivy wasn't laughing along with them as usual. She seemed to sense that Leo's news was serious. "Why don't we let Leo talk," she suggested, focusing her attention on him. "Go ahead, Leo. We're all ears."

"I have something to say that is going to be a bit shocking." He darted a glance in Aunt Ivy and Uncle Jamie's direction. "Kit was just here. She told me some information that will change life as we know it." He paused for a moment. "Ethan is her daughter's father."

Shocked gasps rang out around him at the table.

"No way!" Uncle Jamie said in a raised voice. "That's not true. Ethan would have told us. He wouldn't have walked away from that responsibility."

"He didn't know," Leo said, feeling angry all over again as he said the words out loud. "Kit never told him."

His mother let out a squawk of outrage. "Why did she wait this long to tell us?" she asked, looking at Leo for an answer.

"Ethan was only home once in the year before he died. I don't remember the two of them even hanging out in the same circles," Florence said with a confused expression stamped on her face.

"How do we know she's not lying?" Uncle Patrick asked. Although Leo had always known him as a straight shooter, he chafed at Kit's name being slurred.

"She's not a liar," Leo snapped. "There's no reason why she would say this other than to set things straight. That's not the type of person she is!"

"I believe Kit." The pronouncement from Aunt Ivy appeared to catch all of them by surprise. Leo himself had expected his aunt to be resistant to the news about Ethan being Ada's father. "I know this is going to sound strange, but from the moment I laid eyes on Ada I felt a connection to her. She looks like him. That baby girl has his eyes." She looked over at her husband. "Jamie! That's our grandbaby. I know it deep in my soul. And I'm not giving Kit a pass for what she's done, but I'm prepared to crawl through glass to be a part of Ada's world." She put her head in her hands and began to sob. Leo had no idea if they were tears of joy or sorrow.

"Ivy! That means Ethan left a piece of himself here with us," Jamie said to his wife, throwing his arms around her.

Tears slid down Uncle Jamie's face and he didn't bother trying to wipe them away. "I never imagined this could ever happen in a million years," he said in a choked up voice.

"Neither did I," Aunt Ivy said, dabbing at her eyes with her napkin.

"It's devastating that Ethan didn't know about his child. I have a few choice words for Kit about keeping this secret from us," Uncle Jamie said in an angry tone.

"She's done a terrible thing," Aunt Renata added, scowling.

Leo stood up from the table abruptly, his chair making a banging sound as it clanged against the hardwood floor. As disgusted as he felt about Kit's deception, he couldn't sit by and listen to his family tear her to shreds. "She was scared and alone. The object of town gossip and scorn. She didn't do the right thing, but if you want Ada in your lives, you can't treat Kit like a monster."

Without saying another word, Leo left the house and headed down to the stables. A short while later, Uncle Patrick joined him. "Your mother is sick with worry about you. You know how she gets," Uncle Patrick said in a gruff tone.

Leo kept his head down and didn't look up. He was too afraid that his uncle might see his despair shimmering in his eyes. All he wanted to do at the moment was hide away and lick his wounds, but he had ranching work to do. His work ethic wouldn't allow him to shirk his duties even though it felt as if he was simply going through the motions. His world had gone from vibrant color to shades of gray.

"I'm fine," he said in a clipped voice. "I'm used to being blindsided now. I just wasn't expecting it with Kit."

His uncle let out a ragged sigh. "We all suspected you'd fallen for someone last year and had your heart broken, but we didn't want to pry. Then we lost your dad and we were all reeling from shock and grief." Uncle Patrick narrowed his gaze as he made eye contact with Leo.

"Yeah, you're right. I got my heart trampled by someone I met at a horse auction in Fairbanks then got to know online over the course of a few months." He let out a groan. "I may just be the world's biggest idiot. The woman I thought had feelings for me didn't care at all about me. When I went to meet her the day my father died she stood me up. I wasn't here at the ranch when he needed me the most."

Uncle Patrick ran a hand across his jaw. "So that's why you feel so guilty about not being here when Wes had his attack?"

He let out a groan. "Of course I do," he acknowledged, turning around to face Patrick. "I was off chasing a pipe dream when I could have been saving his life."

Uncle Patrick shook his head. "Leo, I know you like to imagine that was possible, but from what the doctor said, he died in minutes. The seizure led to a stroke. You couldn't have saved him."

"But I—" Leo began before he was cut off.

"Leo!" his uncle snapped. "You've got to face the truth and move on. Wes left us in an instant. There wasn't a thing anyone could have done."

His shoulders sagged and he shut his eyes. The truth hit him like a sledgehammer in the gut. Uncle Patrick was right! His father's life hadn't been in his hands. God was always in control. "You're right. I just have to find a way to accept it.

"And now? With the news about Ethan being Ada's father? It seems to be weighing on you rather heavily. You were awful upset up at the house."

"Honestly, I can't even begin to wrap my head around this bombshell. Keeping a secret like this from Aunt Ivy and Uncle Jamie was cruel."

"And you? How do you feel about Kit not telling you the truth? It seems the two of you have gotten close."

"It makes me angry that I trusted her." He spit the words out. "I thought she was the one. Really. Truly. It hurts, Uncle Patrick. Way more than before. More than I ever imagined it possibly could."

Compassion flared in his uncle's eyes. He patted Leo on the shoulder. "You love her. It's etched all over your face."

He did love her. It was the reason he felt like road-kill right now. It wasn't just a sense of betrayal. Leo loved and adored Kit. She was his everything. When he thought about his future, Kit was there, standing beside him as a huge part of his life. She owned his heart. And it was hard to imagine that ever changing. Try as he might, Leo couldn't just wish these feelings away.

"So is this a deal-breaker? Something you can't live with as a man of faith? Because you know once they got past the shock, Jamie and Ivy are itching to have Ada in their lives."

Leo mulled the questions around in his mind. It seemed impossible to move past this hurt and to pick up the shattered pieces of what they'd been building.

"You don't have to answer me," he continued. "But think about it. Can you stand to let the love of your life go? Put yourself in her shoes. What would you have done?" Leo heard his uncle's boots crunching on the snow as he headed outside. Uncle Patrick's words bounced around in his head like a rubber ball. After realizing he was too distracted to get any more work done, Leo headed to the stables in search of a horse to ride.

Once he'd saddled Lady up, Leo took off across the property at a fierce gallop. He was hoping that if he rode fast enough, he could forget all about a certain green-eyed woman who had caused him more pain than he had ever thought possible.

Christmas Eve was such a blessed night, filled with all the anticipation leading up to Christmas morning. Presents were wrapped, stockings were hung with loving care by the fireplace. Kit tried not to feel sorry for herself, but all she could think about was Leo. There was no question that she'd been uninvited to the Duggans' Christmas Eve get-together. It would have been ridiculous for her to show up when tensions were running so high. She'd texted Leo several times, but he hadn't responded, even though she could see he'd read the message.

In a tough but important move, Kit had sat down with her parents and revealed the truth about Ada's parentage. Their reaction had been one of shock, but they'd been understanding as well.

"We had a feeling there was more to all of this than what you told us," her father had said. "Ethan Duggan was a good man. Ada will grow up knowing her daddy was a hero."

"That will make her proud," her mother had added. "I always pray for the Lord to watch over Adaline. Now I know her father is looking down on her as well and safeguarding her."

Her family was still standing by her. She didn't know what she'd ever done to deserve such unwavering loyalty from them, but she was determined to live up to their belief in her. She planned to do everything in her power to achieve redemption for all her wrongs. Kit knew she would definitely need her faith in the weeks and months to come. The ache of losing Leo and Jupiter had brought Kit to her knees.

God, where are You? I'm so lost. I feel broken. Ashamed. And totally unworthy of the happy ending I dreamed about.

She had no idea how to move forward in her life without Leo. He was everything to her—friend, confidant, encourager. The man she loved. Her everything.

Yes, she loved him. She knew it with a deep certainty that couldn't be shaken. Deeply. Tenderly. A forever type of love. During one of the most stressful periods in her life, Leo had proven himself to be a faithful friend and supporter. He'd been a strong shoulder to lean on and the very reason she was able to work with a service dog. She'd fallen in love with him without even realizing it.

It wasn't hard to see why her feelings had blossomed into love. Leo was such a caring and loyal man. It wasn't likely he would ever feel the same way about her. To him, she was nothing more than a liar. In Leo's eyes, Kit was the person who'd hidden Ada from his family and deceived them all. What if the Duggans hated her? Would Ada somehow feel their animosity toward her and judge Kit for the way she'd mishandled the situation?

Oh, if she could go back in time and do things differently. Kit knew in hindsight that she should have reached out to the Duggans and asked how to contact Ethan overseas. She should have told his family she was pregnant. Shame had stopped her from reaching out to them. Kit hadn't wanted them to think less of her. And all this time later, she was still struggling with feelings of unworthiness.

Lord, I'm Your creation, made in Your image. I'm far from a perfect person and I've made so many mistakes. Please grant me a spirit of peace as I move forward with my life. Grant me the grace to make amends with all those I've harmed.

"Mama." Ada toddled toward her with outstretched hands. Kit smiled down at her little blessing. She'd dressed her in a sweet red-and-white jumpsuit with reindeers scattered across the fabric. Jules had placed a reindeer headband on her, officially making her the most adorable toddler of all time.

"Ada. Who's the cutest reindeer in Alaska?" Kit asked as she scooped her daughter up and rocked her back and forth to the music playing from the speakers in the living room.

"No question she's the prettiest," her father said, walking over and tickling Ada on the belly. The sound of her daughter's tinkling laughter filled the air, providing Kit with a huge dose of cheer. Ever since she'd left the Double D Ranch, Kit's world had been clouded with sadness. Ada was a huge reason to smile through her tears. She wanted to make this Christmas perfect for Ada, despite her own heartache.

Tad came racing over and pushed a few haphaz-
ardly wrapped presents under the Christmas tree. His
enthusiasm made Kit smile. He had already told Kit
his gift to her would be to babysit Ada and to help her
with Jupiter. Love hummed in the air around Kit in her
family home. Through it all, they'd stood beside her
with their unwavering support. And they all loved and
adored Ada, which was the greatest gift of all.

"A group of carolers are coming!" Tad called out as
he peered out the front window.

"Carolers! I thought they weren't making the rounds
this year," her mother said, sounding surprised. "What
a wonderful treat!"

"Everyone grab a sweater so we don't catch cold,"
Jules said as she reached for a knit sweater and began
putting it on her niece.

Carolers were approaching their house. Kit couldn't
help but think that God was trying to lift her up. He
was making sure that she was experiencing joy despite
all her inner turmoil. No matter what was going on
in her personal life, it was still Christmas Eve. After
checking to make sure everyone was warmly dressed,
Kit wrenched open the front door.

A cold wind swept inside, causing Kit to shiver. She
felt her knees wobble the moment her gaze locked on a
pair of soulful hazel eyes. Leo was standing there surrounded by his family members and close friends. Ivy
and Jamie. Florence and the twins. Patrick and Renata.
Ace and Maya. They were all holding white candles
and wearing dark colored cloaks and jackets.

Leo stepped forward so that he was mere inches

away from Kit. Stunned, she took a step away from him. Kit had no idea what was happening. The last time she'd laid eyes on Leo he had been full of condemnation. Now, he was gently smiling at her. She felt a slight push from behind, which moved her closer to Leo. She didn't need to turn around to know it had been Jules who'd nudged her forward.

Before Kit could say a word, the group began to sing "O Holy Night." Overcome with emotion by the beautiful harmonies blended together in song, tears pricked her eyes. "A thrill of hope, the weary world rejoices." Those lyrics had always been so rich and poignant to her. This year the words were even more meaningful. Hope. Could she dare to imagine that Leo and his family had found forgiveness in their hearts for her?

As the song ended, a hushed silence hung in the air.

"W-what are you doing here?" Kit asked as her gaze swept over the group. Leo looked so handsome in his black peacoat, but it almost hurt too much to look at him.

"You said this was your favorite part of Christmas," Leo said, reaching for her hand and gently squeezing it. He was holding her hand?

"Why don't we let Leo and Kit talk in private?" Leo's mother suggested.

"That's a good idea," Jules said. "Come inside from the cold, everyone."

"We don't want to impose," Ivy said, "although I would love to give Ada her Christmas gift." For the first time, Kit noticed she was clutching a gaily wrapped present in her hands.

Jamie put his arm around his wife. "We're thrilled to be grandparents in case you couldn't tell."

"Please don't stand on ceremony," her mother said, beckoning them inside. "After all, we share a grand-daughter."

Everyone moved inside with the exception of Kit and Leo. Once they were alone he asked, "Can we talk outside? You'll need your coat and boots." His voice was filled with so much tenderness it knocked her off balance. He was still holding tightly to her hand. Of all the things she would never have expected this evening, this random visit from Leo and his family sat at the top of the list.

Kit nodded, still too shaken to say much of anything. She turned around and took her long parka off the coat rack, then pushed her feet into her warmest pair of boots. Once she was done, Leo took her hand again and joined it with his.

They stood on her family's wraparound porch, facing each other as the lights from the Christmas tree gleamed from inside the house.

"What's going on?" she asked, looking up at him. "Your family should be screaming at me for what I've done. Instead they're singing carols at my door," she said, shaking her head in disbelief.

"Once the shock and anger wore off, all they wanted to do was thank you for bringing Ada into the world," Leo explained. "They're grateful to be given this un-expected blessing."

It was still so surreal that Ivy and Jamie had for-given her. And Leo! She wanted to pinch herself to make sure he was really standing here on her porch. "I never expected to see you again," she admitted, hurt ringing out in her voice. "You made me believe you couldn't stand the sight of me." It was painful to relive their tense encounter.

Leo clenched his jaw. "I was angry when you told me the truth about Ada. I'm ashamed of the things I said to you and for asking you to leave."

"*You're* ashamed? You've done nothing wrong." She bowed her head. "You have no idea how badly I feel about everything. I failed to do the right thing, and because of my actions, people were hurt. I was way out of line to keep Ada's paternity a secret," Kit said. "So many times I wanted to seek out your family and lay it all bare, but every single time I lost my nerve."

"I understand," Leo said, placing her face between his hands. "You were in a difficult situation, with no direct line to Ethan. And then when he met Rebecca and got engaged to her, you didn't want to disrupt his life."

"You have no idea how much I wish I had," she admitted. "It would have spared everyone so much pain."

He swept his palm across her cheek. "You were wounded too. Pregnant and facing single motherhood alone. Dealing with gossip and scorn. Everyone knows you didn't have it easy."

"Most people in Owl Creek were kind to me. So many were supportive and gave me advice about raising a baby. I even had a little baby shower at Tea Time, so it wasn't all bad." She wrinkled her nose. "But there were a few stinkers who really made me feel unworthy of bringing a life into the world."

A hissing sound escaped from his lips. "If I'd known, I would have dealt with them on your behalf. I never wanted to stand in judgment of you when I found out about you and Ethan, but I did." Leo winced. "You were caught in a terrible predicament. Because of circumstances, all the shame and embarrassment were placed on your back to carry around. You bore all of it with grace and courage. And you did so while raising the most wonderful little girl."

No one had ever said that to her before. Not in those words. Suddenly, she felt ten feet tall.

"And that's just one of the reasons why I love you, Kit O'Malley," Leo added. "I promise you there are dozens more."

A squeak came from somewhere deep inside her. *Love?* Had Leo really declared his love for her? "You're going to have to say that again, because I feel like I might be dreaming," Kit said in a low voice.

"I'm in love with you, Kit. Head over heels. Over the moon. Totally smitten. Because of you I've been able to step out on a limb of faith and believe in the redeeming power of love. I honestly never thought I'd get to this place again." He locked gazes with her. When she looked into his eyes, Kit saw nothing but love shimmering back at her.

Kit raised a trembling hand to her mouth. "Leo, I never imagined you would love me... All this time my own feelings for you have been building and soaring. I love you too. So very much." She raised herself on her tippy-toes and placed a kiss on his lips. Kit wrapped her arms around his neck and pulled him close.

When the kiss ended, Leo held Kit in his arms as her head rested against his chest. He ran his fingers lovingly through her hair. "The past is the past, Kit," Leo said. "All I care about is walking a path together toward our future. You, me and Ada."

"Oh, Leo. You've made this the best Christmas Eve ever," Kit gushed.

"Thank you for loving me," Leo whispered in her ear as he placed tender kisses on the side of her face.

She put her hands on his chest and gazed up at him. "We should go inside now. I owe your family an explanation that only I can give," Kit said, inhaling a deep breath. "It won't be easy, but it's something that I need to do so we can all move forward. I want to redeem myself in their eyes."

"They'll appreciate that. I know they have some questions," Leo said. "I'll be right beside you, baby. You've got this!" He linked his hand with hers as they headed inside, united in their love for one another and a desire to achieve healing for their families.

On Christmas morning, Leo woke up to a whole new world. Reconciling with Kit and bridging the gap between her and his family made the holiday even more special. He knew Ethan was smiling down at all of them from Heaven. Just knowing that Kit loved him was the best present Leo had ever received. The shadows of the past had been vanquished. He now knew that this love was stronger than anything he'd ever dared to dream about having.

Today, he and Kit, along with their families, would start making memories.

His family met up with the O'Malleys at church for a lovely morning service. Beautiful hymns streamed from the sanctuary, filling the space with music. Afterward, they all gathered at the Duggans' home in order to allow Ethan's loved ones to experience their first Christmas with Ada. The mood among the families was celebratory. Everyone expressed gratitude for reconciliation and redemption. Ada seemed to readily accept her newfound grandparents. As Kit said, there would be more love in the little girl's life and who didn't need more hugs and kisses?

"I'm so thankful for all of this, Leo," Kit said, looking around the living room where they'd all gathered to watch the twins and Ada open their presents.

"Let's go give Jupiter his gift. I miss him," Kit said, grabbing Leo by the hand and leading him outside where Jupiter was running around with Daisy. They were racing around in the snow and making toys out of sticks.

"Jupiter," Kit called out before letting out a high-pitched whistle. "Come on, boy."

Jupiter raced to her side, full of excitement to be reunited with her. He was wagging his tail so fast and furiously it made her giggle.

"Just so you know, Leo, you're not the only one I've fallen in love with," Kit said playfully.

"Oh, really?" Leo asked. His brows knit together. "Do I have some competition?"

She wrapped her arms around Jupiter's neck and kissed his forehead. "I love this guy here more than I can ever put into words."

"You don't need to say a word, Kit. It's written all over your face," Leo said, grinning.

The sound of a honking horn rang out just as a van pulled up in the driveway.

"Oh, how wonderful," Kit said, clapping her hands together. "Your Christmas present is here."

Leo squinted at the van. "Is that Ace? What's he doing here?"

Kit rubbed her hands together. "Wait for it," she said, walking toward the van and greeting Ace as he stepped out of the vehicle. "Hey, Ace. Thanks for coming out here on Christmas."

"No worries. Merry Christmas," Ace said with a grin. "Anything for my best friend's girl."

"Word travels fast," Leo said with a smile. He liked the sound of Kit being his girl.

Ace moved toward the back of the van and opened it up. Within seconds, two leashed puppies with big red bows on their necks—a German shepherd and Labrador retriever—came into view.

"Surprise!" Kit cried out, raising her hands in the air.

Leo stood with his mouth halfway open, staring at the two pups.

"He looks surprised all right," Ace said with a chuckle. "I'm going to head back to town before Maya begins blowing up my cell phone. We're having Christmas dinner with our folks."

"Thanks again, Ace," Kit called out. "Merry Christmas!"

Leo waved at Ace before turning toward Kit. "Two dogs, huh?"

"I know how much you enjoy training service animals. And pretty soon you're going to have to hand Jupiter over to me, so this will keep you busy. There are so many people who could benefit from your services. Not to mention the fact that these dogs needed a home."

"How long have you been planning this?" Leo asked.

"It actually all came together in the last week. I almost canceled after we had our falling out, but Ace told me to keep the faith." She bit her lip. "Is this okay? I hope you're happy about having new pups to train. Are you?"

"Yeah, I'm happy," he said, his voice tight with emotion. "No one but you could have figured out that this is what I've been wanting for a while now. My service dog training program transformed into more than a way to honor my dad. It's a pathway to help others and to honor the abilities of these very special animals. And I'll always think of it as the thing that brought the two of us together. That makes it very special indeed."

"Not just the two of us," Kit said with a chuckle, darting a glance in Jupiter's direction. "I'll always be thankful for both of you."

Leo swept Kit into his arms and pressed a kiss on

her lips as Jupiter began chasing around his newfound fur buddies.

"This is what happens when you believe," Kit whispered against his lips. "All of your dreams come true."

Epilogue

One year later at Christmas

Snow was gently falling at the Duggan ranch, blanketing the property in a winter flurry of the fluffy white stuff. Twinkling lights dotted the stretch of road leading to the homestead. Inside the barn, family members and townsfolk were gathered to celebrate the most joyful event of the season—Kit and Leo's holiday wedding. To Kit, it seemed as if the entire town of Owl Creek had come to witness the ceremony. Leo had arranged for her to be brought to the ranch in a horse-drawn carriage. A perfect Cinderella moment.

The interior of the barn had been transformed into a winter wonderland by both of their families. White poinsettia flowers, strings of white lights and a carpet of rose petals leading to the altar all created a romantic ambiance. Red bows had been attached to every chair and bench, providing a burst of color. Love hummed and pulsed in the air around them.

Jupiter, decked out in a white service vest, led Kit down the aisle along with her father. Leo stood at the altar, beaming with joy as he waited for Kit to reach his side. Ace was beside him as best man while Jules held Ada in her arms as she served as maid of honor.

After Kit and Leo were pronounced man and wife, Leo dipped his head down and placed a triumphant kiss on his bride's lips. "Forever," Kit murmured, knowing she would be by Leo's side for the rest of their days.

"This is the day which the Lord hath made; we will rejoice and be glad in it." Leo uttered the words to Kit as he joined hands with her and walked toward the doors of the barn to rousing applause. Ace and Braden had tied cans and streamers to the back of his truck, as well as a Just Married sign. Leo held Kit's hand and helped her into the truck before he sat down behind the wheel and drove them down the road toward the house.

The reception was being held at the homestead where everyone was gathering to celebrate the bride and groom's union. The mood was one of pure joy and contentment. All of their loved ones were there, surrounding them with love and support. Halfway through the party, Leo and Kit snuck outside to get a glimpse of the spectacular moon.

"Look!" Leo said, pointing up to the sky. "Did you see that? A snowy owl just flew past. It looked like the owl's wings were touching the moon."

"Breathtaking," Kit said, her eyes looking upward toward the heavens. Her vision hadn't declined too much over the past year, which gave her hope about her treatments. She could still see the sun shining in the sky, the town's famous owls soaring up above and Ada's precious little face. Kit was blessed.

"Truly stunning," Leo said as his gaze focused on Kit, grazing the side of her cheek with his knuckles. "My beautiful Alaskan bride. God has been so good to me. I've never been more content than I am right now."

"I can't even put into words how happy I am," Kit gushed. "And I'm thankful for all of our blessings. You were able to see past the truth about Adaline's parentage and forgive me for keeping such a huge secret."

Leo smiled at her. "In the end, it was easy. You came into my life when I'd given up on love. It was like finding a diamond in a sea of glass."

"God always had a plan for us. We just had to be patient and wait for Him to point us in the right direction." Kit squeezed his hand with all her might. She knew he'd been through an emotional journey before they'd fallen in love. Despite his losses and a crushing betrayal, he'd still opened his heart up to her. He had stepped out on a limb of faith and chosen to believe in her and their love.

"My heart ached to find my other half," Leo continued, "but instead I fell for something that wasn't real. It blinded me. Until you came into my life and showed me all of the possibilities stretched out before me. I am blessed beyond measure."

"You saw me, Leo. Through all my anxiety and fear about losing my sight, you were able to encourage and inspire me." She choked back raw emotion. "You're going to be a great father for Ada."

"I'll always be there for our family. You, me and

Ada, as well as any other children we might be blessed with. I want to teach Ada all about Ethan, but at the same time I want to stand in for him and be that father figure. That's what I want more than anything."

"Oh, Leo. That means so much to me. When I came to the ranch that first morning, I had so little hope in my heart, yet you stood by my side and showed me the path. You believed in me."

Leo placed Kit's face between his hands. "And I always will. If you ever lose your way, I'll help steer you in the right direction."

"And I'll always do the same for you," she vowed.

Kit rested her head against his chest, firm in the knowledge that she had found her forever. She would continue her training with Jupiter and her husband, so she would be fully prepared if her sight deteriorated even further. She was living in love. All her fears had been replaced with joy and anticipation for the future. All the shadows had disappeared, leaving nothing but sunlight.

* * * * *

*If you enjoyed this story, look for
these other books by Belle Calhoune:*

Their Alaskan Past
Hiding in Alaska
Alaska Christmas Redemption
An Alaskan Twin Surprise

Dear Reader,

Thank you for joining me on this inspirational journey to Owl Creek, Alaska. I truly enjoyed crafting Kit and Leo's friends-to-romance love story. Kit and Leo are both at a crossroads in their lives. Kit's medical diagnosis is devastating. She's filled with fear about her future and how she'll navigate her world. Leo has been steeped in grief and recovering from heartbreak. He's emotionally bruised. Jupiter, Kit's incredible service dog, is a symbol of hope for Kit as she learns to accept her impending vision loss. Along the way, their platonic feelings morph into romance.

Faith is a major theme of this story. I love how Kit and Leo lean on their faith when their lives get difficult. Without it, both would be lost. Their spiritual strengths sustain them.

As a dog lover, researching and writing about service dogs was an incredible experience. Jupiter is a Labrador retriever. I've had several as pets and they are incredibly loyal and amiable. Jupiter works hard and he has a huge heart. This pup will serve Kit well in her future and help her lead a full life.

As always, writing for the Love Inspired line is a privilege. Working in my pj's and being able to hang out with my dogs are huge perks of being an author. I love hearing from readers, however you choose to reach out to me. I can be found on my Author Belle Calhoune Facebook page, my bellecalhoune.com website and on Instagram @BelleCalhoune.

Blessings,
Belle

Get 4 FREE REWARDS!

We'll send you 2 FREE Books plus 2 FREE Mystery Gifts.

FREE Value Over **$20**

Both the **Love Inspired®** and **Love Inspired® Suspense** series feature compelling novels filled with inspirational romance, faith, forgiveness, and hope.

YES! Please send me 2 FREE novels from the Love Inspired or Love Inspired Suspense series and my 2 FREE gifts (gifts are worth about $10 retail). After receiving them, if I don't wish to receive any more books, I can return the shipping statement marked "cancel." If I don't cancel, I will receive 6 brand-new Love Inspired Larger-Print books or Love Inspired Suspense Larger-Print books every month and be billed just $6.24 each in the U.S. or $6.49 each in Canada. That is a savings of at least 17% off the cover price. It's quite a bargain! Shipping and handling is just 50¢ per book in the U.S. and $1.25 per book in Canada.* I understand that accepting the 2 free books and gifts places me under no obligation to buy anything. I can always return a shipment and cancel at any time by calling the number below. The free books and gifts are mine to keep no matter what I decide.

Choose one: ☐ **Love Inspired**
Larger-Print
(122/322 IDN GRDF)

☐ **Love Inspired Suspense**
Larger-Print
(107/307 IDN GRDF)

Name (please print)

Address _____ Apt. #

City _____ State/Province _____ Zip/Postal Code

Email: Please check this box ☐ if you would like to receive newsletters and promotional emails from Harlequin Enterprises ULC and its affiliates. You can unsubscribe anytime.

Mail to the Harlequin Reader Service:
IN U.S.A.: P.O. Box 1341, Buffalo, NY 14240-8531
IN CANADA: P.O. Box 603, Fort Erie, Ontario L2A 5X3

Want to try 2 free books from another series! Call 1-800-873-8635 or visit www.ReaderService.com.

---

*Terms and prices subject to change without notice. Prices do not include sales taxes, which will be charged (if applicable) based on your state or country of residence. Canadian residents will be charged applicable taxes. Offer not valid in Quebec. This offer is limited to one order per household. Books received may not be as shown. Not valid for current subscribers to the Love Inspired or Love Inspired Suspense series. All orders subject to approval. Credit or debit balances in a customer's account(s) may be offset by any other outstanding balance owed by or to the customer. Please allow 4 to 6 weeks for delivery. Offer available while quantities last.

Your Privacy—Your information is being collected by Harlequin Enterprises ULC, operating as Harlequin Reader Service. For a complete summary of the information we collect, how we use this information and to whom it is disclosed, please visit our privacy notice located at corporate.harlequin.com/privacy-notice. From time to time we may also exchange your personal information with reputable third parties. If you wish to opt out of this sharing of your personal information, please visit readerservice.com/consumerschoice or call 1-800-873-8635. **Notice to California Residents**—Under California law, you have specific rights to control and access your data. For more information on these rights and how to exercise them, visit corporate.harlequin.com/california-privacy.

LIRLIS22R2

HARLEQUIN
PLUS

Announcing a **BRAND-NEW** multimedia subscription service for romance fans like you!

Read, Watch and Play.

Experience the easiest way to get the romance content you crave.

Start your **FREE 7 DAY TRIAL** at www.harlequinplus.com/freetrial.

Inspired by true events,
The Secret Society of Salzburg
is a gripping and heart-wrenching story of
two very different women united to bring
light to the darkest days of World War II.

Don't miss this thrilling and uplifting page-turner
from bestselling author

RENEE RYAN

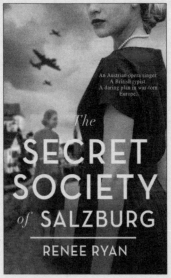

"A gripping, emotional story of courage and strength,
filled with extraordinary characters."
—*New York Times* bestselling author **RaeAnne Thayne**

Coming soon from Love Inspired!

LOVE INSPIRED
LoveInspired.com